Veblen

—

A Charlie LeBeau Mystery

Gregory L. Heitmann

For my Grandma, Betty Jean Hagen.

A Charlie LeBeau Mystery

Many thanks to my family, gracias!

As always, a big thank you to my editor:

Gwyneth

Front cover design by: Gregory L. Heitmann based on *The Moving Art of Manfred Schatz*

Back cover photo credits: USDA, Google Earth, and the author

A Charlie LeBeau Mystery

Author's Note

This is a work of fiction and the usual rules apply. The characters, the conversations, and the incidents portrayed in this novel have been invented by the author. Nothing in this book is to be construed as real. Any resemblance to actual events, or persons, whether living or dead, is coincidental. Again, none of the characters are real. This is a fictional story conceived for entertainment purposes only.

A Charlie LeBeau Mystery

Other novels by Gregory L. Heitmann:

Fort Sisseton – Dakota Territory

Chief Red Iron – The Lakota Uprising

The G MANN 2 – Pay-2-Play

Teener Baseball

Long Hollow – A Charlie LeBeau Mystery

Buffalo Lake – A Charlie LeBeau Mystery

Big Coulee – A Charlie LeBeau Mystery

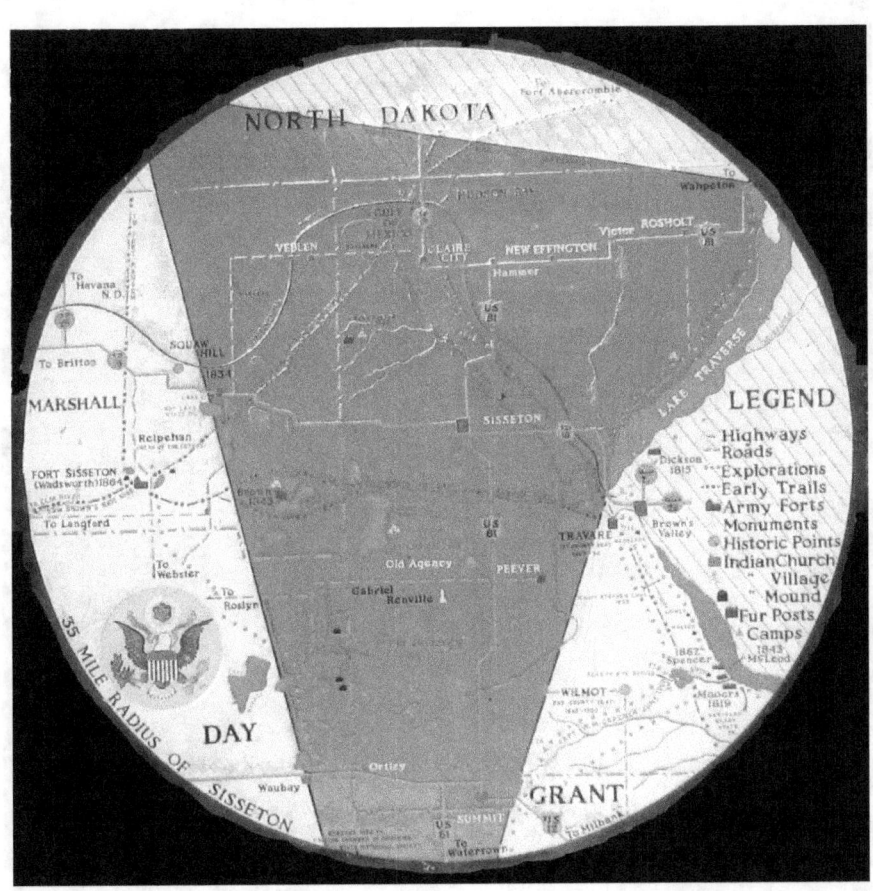

Sisseton Area Map

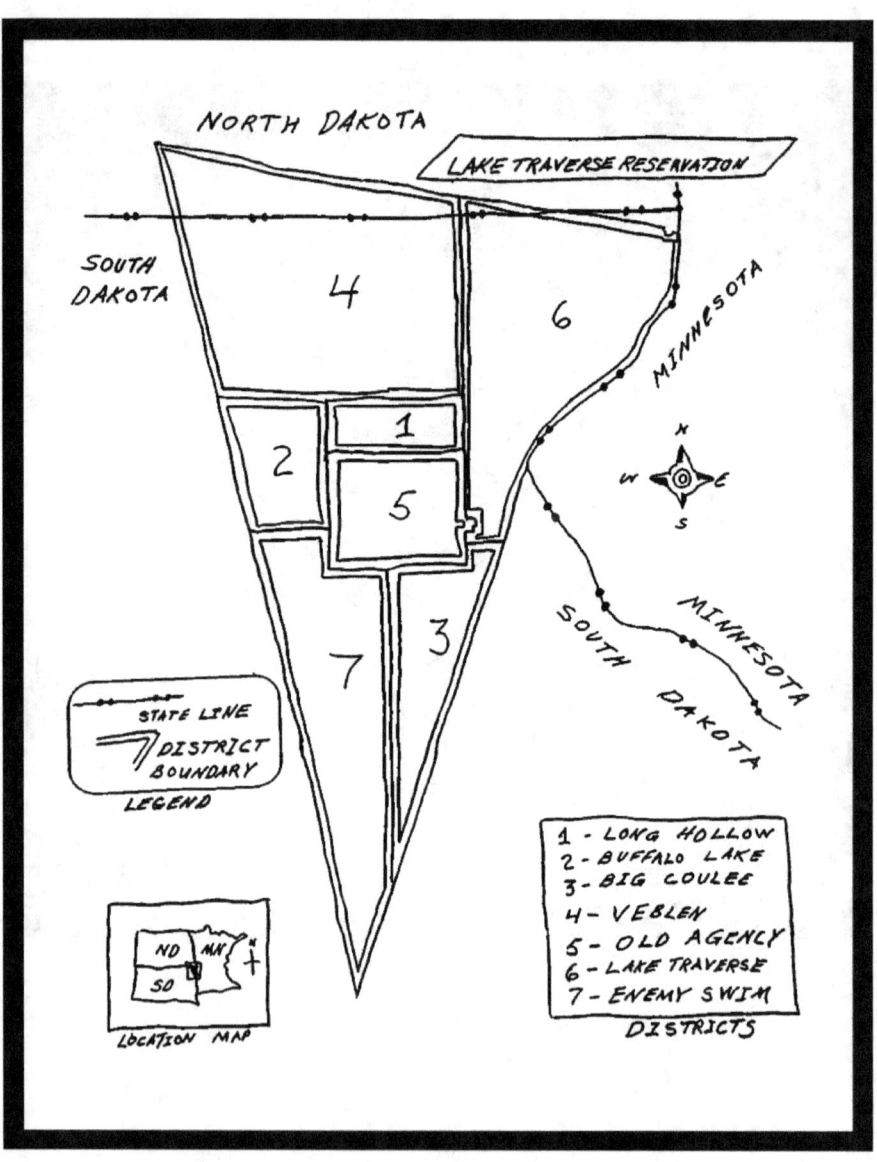

Lake Traverse Indian Reservation Districts

Chapter 1
Twin Cities

Bloomington, Minnesota – Present Day

The neon "VACANCY" light buzzes loudly beneath the Wayfarer Motel sign printed vertically in foot-high lettering. Three cars are scattered in the dimly lit parking lot. The highway noise combines with the jets from the Minneapolis-St. Paul Airport to form a dull roar.

Two twin beds fill up the tiny motel room. The street din and airport jets are a faint hiss inside the rented room competing against the fan of the air conditioner. A man in each bed prepares for sleep. Between them a night stand with a dim bulb strains to illuminate the room. A nearly empty pint bottle of cheap vodka, generic brand, rests on its side next to the light. The man in the bed closest to the interior of the room, drifts off then wakes with a start and reaches for the bottle on the night stand.

Charlie LeBeau looks up from his book toward the man grasping clumsily at the bottle. "You ok?"

Charlie LeBeau is forty five years old, but could easily pass for thirty. The Bureau of Indian Affairs Police Sergeant looks more like a French television news anchor than his Lakota heritage lets on. His French surname a reflection of his outward appearance. He is in excellent physical condition, but he is worn down after eight days on the road with his hunting partner. Not a sportsman's hunt. This is a man hunt. Charlie's partner is his friend, Federal Bureau of Investigation Special Agent Austin Brown.

Brown takes a small sip of the vodka, his mouth burns. He grunts the words, "I'm going to kill that man."

He guzzles the remaining vodka in the bottle. He struggles for a moment threading the cap loosely on the bottle before dropping it off the bed onto the floor. Groaning he rolls to his side, curling up in his sheets. Austin Brown is a young, real-life version of the Tommy Lee Jones marquee character in the movie *The Fugitive*. His rugged face with chiseled jaw is a dominating feature that provides a tough, serious appearance that commands authority. It's a perfect fit for his mostly humorless personality.

Charlie is back to his book and in less than two minutes, soft snores of sleep emanate from the other bed. Charlie looks to his partner in the dim light. It's more than a worry. It is a nightly ritual for Austin, a self medicated-vodka-induced sleep. It's been that way for two months.

Chapter 2
Pierre, South Dakota

Two Months Ago – Pierre, South Dakota

Pierre, South Dakota, the state capitol, is nestled along the Mighty Mo, the Missouri River. It is ten or so miles downstream from one of the largest earthen dams in the world, Oahe Dam. The area is steeped in history. Long before the Lewis and Clark Expedition, numerous bands of Lakota inhabited the area. Reservation lands were flooded by the Oahe Reservoir; once again, in a slight to the native peoples, another in the long line of broken promises to the Indians, they were once again forced by the American government to relocate, chased by the dammed water.

Nonetheless, it is a beautiful area, the big river, slicing South Dakota in half. The western half of the state predominantly prairie and grazing for cattle, and the eastern half is fertile, tilled cropland. The dichotomy of the glacial ages. The eastern side of the state's prolific farmland is the product of the most recent glacial efforts. The "West River," area of South Dakota, as it is known, missed the last round of glaciation. The soil is less churned and thus less fertile. The lines of the glacial retreat can be seen in the rivers that run west to east emptying into the Missouri. From south to north you'll find the White River, the Bad River, the Cheyenne River, the Little Moreau River, and the Grand River, all benchmarks marking the dissolution of the glacier that finally disappeared to the north ten thousand years ago.

Today, the Capitol City is a quiet town of about fourteen thousand people resting on the east side of the river. Directly across the Missouri River on US Highway 14, over the Lieutenant Commander John C. Waldron Bridge, Fort Pierre adds another two thousand people to the area's population.

Downtown Pierre is marked by the largest building in the city, the Federal Building. It houses the post office, the federal courthouse, and on the fifth and top floor, the Federal Bureau of Investigation. Agent Austin Brown sits at his desk overlooking a view to the west with the Missouri River just a half-mile away. The FBI-man is lost in thought for the moment as the day draws to its end. He sees the traffic on West Sioux Avenue below him start and stop at the signal lights. This is the main thoroughfare of Pierre, a combination of US Highway 14 and South Dakota Highway 34.

Brown's thoughts harken back to one of his most recently completed cases in Sisseton, South Dakota. It was a brutal case involving a Catholic priest, abuse, and organized crime operating out of the Twin Cities. He still can't believe it sometimes, this life in South Dakota, a place that might as well have been the moon for him as he grew up in Cleveland, Ohio. He realizes his life is comfortable; it is a far cry from his upbringing. Even with the crime on the Indian reservations, life in small town South Dakota is bucolic. His family is safely tucked away from the hustle and bustle of metropolitan areas.

In the distance, toward the Fort Pierre side of the river, Austin strains his eyes trying to make out the Verendrye Memorial. It is a fascination for Austin. To think about this jewel of an area and its layered history, it is hard to imagine. The Verendrye Memorial is a monument marking history. The granite memorial erected by the State Historical Society and Fort Pierre Commercial Club in 1933 is simply etched with these words: *"Here on March 30, 1743 the Verendryes buried a lead tablet to claim this region for France. This tablet was found on Feb. 16, 1913 is the first written record of the visit of White Men to South Dakota."*

If anyone ever visits, Austin insists on taking them to the Verendrye Memorial site. It never fails to leave the visitors amazed that two French brothers trekked the Missouri some three-hundred-fifty-plus years ago.

His eyes scan the river. He smiles to himself as he thinks of his family's new pastime, fishing. Never one for the outdoors, he finally broke down and got some inexpensive rods and reels along with rudimentary tackle. To the surprise of everyone, they enjoyed the expedition to the tailrace, the area where the water spills from the dam after spinning the hydroelectric components. The tailrace area is a place where even the most amateur fisherman can have success. In their first trip they caught walleye, trout, and one northern pike the size of the youngest daughter's arm. They were hooked on fishing.

17

Brown's musings are halted as he flinches to the ring and flashing LED on his phone. "Agent Brown," he answers in his professional tone.

"Hey, Honey," Jeannie Brown coos over her Bluetooth phone connection and Brown relaxes. Jeannie reaches for the radio volume knob, lowering the sound of the Jay & the Americans' song "Come a Little Bit Closer."

The oldies radio disc jockey announces, "Let's do a double-play!" Jay & the Americans return to the speakers with "Cara Mia."

Jeannie Brown, wife of Austin Brown and mother of his two children, is forty years old. She is a full-time mother of the two grade-schoolers and she is in her mini-van on the way to retrieve them from school. Jeanie is the prototype All-American girl. Plainly attractive with long sandy-brown hair in a ponytail, she talks as she drives. Tan and tone, she gets a workout with the kids, and while the kids are in school, she trains for triathlons. Her tank top lets everyone see that she is in good shape.

"What's up?" Austin asks, voice picking up.

"Just calling to tell you to make sure you are home for dinner. Pork Chops for supper. I'm just leaving Lynn's. I'm going to pick up the kids."

Austin is up from his desk. He walks to the north side of the building to try to catch a glimpse of Jeannie in her van. He smiles to himself. "Don't worry, I'll be there. Nothing going on here."

Jeannie pulls out of Lynn's Dakotamart onto South Central Avenue and heads across the railroad tracks. She heads northeast and enters the intersection of West Pleasant Drive. She is oblivious to the speeding pickup truck that crushes her driver's side door, pushing the van onto its side. It is as violent of a crash as one can imagine. The truck, reaching fifty miles per hour at impact, is a missile.

As Austin casually walks to get a view from the north side of the building he can hear the crash, Jeannie's scream, and her muffled groans. He stops for a moment. "Jeannie? Jeannie?" Austin is confused. He pulls the phone away to look at the screen, unsure of his connection. He bolts to the windows to get a view of the street below. He can see the crashed vehicles as he repeats, "Jeannie? Jeannie?"

The door of the 1970's three-quarter ton, four-wheel drive Ford, an old ranch truck, swings open. A man emerges stiffly from the wrecked, steaming vehicle. He removes a motorcycle helmet and tosses it into the bed of the truck. The man walking away in jeans and leather jacket ambles off, as if nothing happened, his stride becoming more casual as he dismisses the impact of the wreck. "Jeannie!" Austin is screaming into his phone as the flood of recognition washes over him. "Jeannie!"

He bolts for the elevators, but chooses the stairs instead of waiting. Rage cascades over Austin. The man is Elliot Kauffman, the Deer Slayer, and he is walking away from the crash, once again escaping his grasp.

Chapter 3
Unstable

Avera St. Mary's Hospital – Pierre, South Dakota

Just outside the intensive care unit, Austin listens as a doctor explains his wife's condition. The doctor is dressed in scrubs and speaks in a matter-of-fact tone, "We had to remove her spleen. It's not an uncommon injury in this kind of trauma. Stopped the internal bleeding. Her broken leg and arm are going to require more surgery. She's lucky. These new-generation side curtain air bags did a good job protecting her head and neck." Austin nods along to the doctor's words. "We got her stabilized for the moment." The doctor puts a hand on Austin's shoulder.

"Does she need to get to Sioux Falls?" Austin questions.

The doctor shakes his head. "She's not out of the woods yet. I'm not going to try to move her."

"Can I see her?" Austin's eyes plead with his words.

"She's not going to respond. We put her into her a drug induced coma."

"I just want to sit with her."

The doctor concedes. "I'll tell the nurse to let you in."

*   *   *

The interior ICU room is a wall of computers and monitors. Wires trail every which way from Jeannie's body. Austin sits next to the bed holding his wife's hand. He whispers, "He's a dead man. He just doesn't know it yet."

Tears fall from the man's eyes. His helplessness takes him back to his childhood for an instant, but he wipes his eyes and returns to his stoic persona. After a half hour with his wife, he pushes his chair back as a nurse enters to tend to the patient. "You can stay," the nurse assures him.

"No, I have to make a phone call."

Austin exits the room, pulling his cell phone from his jacket pocket. He notices his gray suit coat sleeve is smeared with blood, dried now, staining through to his shirt. It is his wife's blood and it crumbles between his fingers, flaking away as he rubs it. He had been able to comfort her as she was pinned in the car. Jeannie had regained consciousness and Austin had been by her side. They had been able to exchange their vows of love for each other as she hung upside down, suspended by the seatbelt in excruciating pain.

The decision to stay by his wife's side had come at a cost. It was a decision foregoing any pursuit of the Deer Slayer at the time, but now it consumes him. The thoughts of his wife and revenge bounce back and forth in his brain. It's about to become his life's purpose...getting the man that attacked his wife.

Chapter 4
Early Call

Charlie's Manufactured Home – Sisseton, South Dakota

Charlie, Claude, and Nat are at the front door as Veronica clears the breakfast dishes. It's six o'clock in the morning, an indecent hour for the weekend unless you are hunting, and this Saturday it is another weekend of the fall turkey season. "Bye. Be careful," Veronica calls out from the kitchen over the soft sounds of the Ozark Mountain Daredevils' song "Jackie Blue." The men are in head-to-toe camo, shuffling to the door as Charlie's phone buzzes in his pocket. He digs for the device. "Who'd be calling at this hour?"

Claude holds up his hands and lets loose with a sarcastic tongue, "Let's see, you're a cop...I'm guessing it's your boss and it's crime related."

Nat holds back a laugh. "Nope, you're wrong," Charlie sneers. He holds up the screen toward his dad. "It's Agent Brown." Charlie waves them toward the door. "I gotta take this. You guys go. I'll catch up."

Nat and Claude head out the door as Charlie pushes the accept call button. "Agent Brown, this better be good, I'm heading out the door to shoot a turkey."

Charlie hears only silence, maybe some heavy breathing. It's uncomfortable enough to cause Charlie to repeat a questioning, "Hello?"

"I'm sorry to bother you, Charlie," Austin's voice is stoic and monotone, although Charlie is used to this from the man; there is a weakness to it.

"What is it? What's wrong?"

The concern in Charlie's voice halts Veronica in her tracks as she wipes down the table and catches Charlie's eye. Charlie signals her with a shrug, not understanding the call.

"I need your help," Austin's voice is low, and Charlie strains to hear.

"Agent Brown? What is it? I can barely hear you."

Charlie can hear Austin clear his throat and the words are clear and forceful now, "It's the Deer Slayer. He just tried to kill my wife."

The silence is deafening to Charlie as the words sink in. "Whoa. What do you mean?"

"I'm going to kill that man," Austin drawls the words slowly, rage building in each syllable.

"Austin, I don't understand." Charlie's breathing shortens. "Tell me, what is going on?"

"It's Elliot. He just rammed my wife in her minivan. She's in the hospital. She's in rough shape. They don't know..." the words trail away. Charlie can hear a deep breath and the snuffling sounds of man holding back tears.

"What do you need from me? The kids? Are your kids ok?"

Austin's voice is trance-like, repeating the details. "She has a broken arm, broken leg. They had to remove her spleen. She's sedated. They don't want to move her yet. They're talking Sioux Falls."

"I'll head out now. You want me out to come out there?" Charlie questions.

Austin rambles more details in his monotone, "I saw him Charlie. I saw Elliot walk away from the crash. He was wearing a motorcycle helmet. The police told me the truck he was driving was reported stolen from Lower Brule four days ago. He was plotting this. She had called me. Pork Chops. That's what we were going to have for supper. Kids are with her friend Wendy. I'm at the hospital. She was just on her way to pick them up from school."

"Thank God," Charlie whispers the words, acknowledging the status of the kids. "You're sure? This is Elliot?"

"I already got the video from a security camera at an Insurance agency as the Deer Slayer casually walked down the street. It's him."

Austin's voice is strong again. "I need your help, Charlie. Can you come to Pierre? You know this guy. I need your help."

"I'll pack right now." Charlie points to Veronica and she points at herself. "You want me to bring Veronica? Maybe she could look after the kids?"

"No, Jeannie's mom is on the way. Flying in from Indiana. She'll be here tonight." Austin breathes deeply, "You gotta tell Veronica he's out there. She may be in danger. Get Skip to get her some protection. Tell Claude and Nat. They need to be on the lookout." His voice is a growl now, "It's only a matter of time, Charlie. I'm going to kill that man."

Charlie is silent. He is suddenly hyperaware and can hear his own shallow breaths. "Austin, I'm on my way. We'll talk about it when I get there."

Chapter 5
Internal Injuries

Charlie's trip from Sisseton in northeast South Dakota to the center of the state is a meandering journey mostly on empty highway. The four hour drive gives him plenty of time to ponder the abruptness of the situation. Time goes by and memories fade, but the Deer Slayer back in his life feels like it was just yesterday. Charlie feels guilty. He knows it could have easily been him asking for Agent Brown's help. He shudders at the thought of his complacency and the risk that was there, and is there now. Everyone is on high alert now, Elliot's presence is known. The Deer Slayer's element of surprise is gone.

It's an emotional overload; that's the way Charlie categorizes all of this. He recognizes that it has to be a business-like approach. One has to try to keep the feelings in check, stick with facts. "Easier said than done," Charlie whispers to himself. His mind continues to mull over the circumstances. John Conlee's song "Rose-Colored Glasses" fades and is replaced by the classic country music stylings of Johnny Paycheck and his tune "The Only Hell My Mama Ever Raised." The music draws Charlie's attention and he clicks off the radio to think in silence. It's beginning to sink in...the actuality of the situation. He argues within his conscience as he drives. Half his brain argues everything will be fine, the other half forecasts doom and gloom.

South on US Highway 83 and then turning west on US Highway 14, Charlie is in the homestretch to Pierre. Straight to the hospital, that is the plan. Try to provide some reassurance to Agent Brown, and then make arrangements and a plan of attack. It sounds simple enough in his head as he drives.

There is no way to be prepared for the scene Charlie walks into at the hospital. The rushing doctors and nurses choreographed into and out of the ICU remind him of a ballet. It is pure adrenaline in the hallway surrounding Jeanine's room. A nurse is holding both of Agent Brown's arms, trying to keep him out of the way, shielding the door to the ICU. Charlie takes over the job of restraint. "I'm here, Austin. Let them do their jobs," Charlie tries to provide a modicum of assurance.

"Something went wrong." Agent Brown strains to look into the room as the doctor and nurses work. "The alarms started going off."

*   *   *

It is surreal for Charlie. He holds his arm around Agent Brown as the doctor attempts to explain. The doctor is youthful looking. He seems way too young to be trained in medicine. He wears scrubs and his jet black beard is neatly trimmed. "I'm sorry," the doctor repeats for the fourth time. "Her internal organs were bruised. It was a tough call. We think she had a blood clot to her heart causing cardiac arrest. We couldn't revive her. She's gone."

The doctor puts a hand on Agent Brown's shoulder. Charlie can see the stunned expression on the face of the young doctor. It's a look of bewilderment that he has seen from doctors before. It is a look of disbelief that they can't save the patient, even with all their training and confidence. "How could this patient die on me? Me! A skilled doctor?" Charlie had seen that look in the emergency room many a time after a car crash.

Charlie's memory flashes back to his own experience of hearing the news from the doctor, most recently his sister, dead from cancer just a couple years ago. Twenty years ago, the same for his mother. Charlie had also delivered the bad news to families, informing their loved ones that so-and-so had been killed in a crash. Surreal. That's the only word that comes to mind for Charlie as all these thoughts flash through his head in an instant as he tries to hold up Agent Brown.

Agent Brown's body shudders. He can't stay on his feet and Charlie holds him as he eases the man to the wall for support. Brown braces against the wall, and Charlie loosens his grip as he watches him slide down the wall, his body wracked with sobs. Charlie kneels and wraps his arms around the wailing man. Pushing Agent Brown's head to his shoulder and absorbing the crying spasms he attempts to provide comfort.

Chapter 6
Almanac

Twin Cities – Present Day

The room at the Wayfarer Motel has been the headquarters for the two men for the last five days. The trail has brought them here. The cheap motel is sufficient for their needs, a place to sleep at night. The digital clock on the nightstand between the two beds shows 1:30 am in its red numbers. Charlie is in the bed closest to the window. He bookmarks his well read copy of Aldo Leopold's *Sand County Almanac*. It is his go-to book for calm in stressful times. The dim light on the nightstand struggles to illuminate the room. Charlie sighs, "It's been ten days, Agent Brown. We are getting nowhere."

"Come on, Charlie," Austin whines from his bed closest to the interior of the room. He takes a slug from the bottle, emptying the clear liquid. "You can call me Austin. I'm not Agent Brown anymore."

His words are slurred. He clumsily screws the cap on the liquor pint, taking a full minute and all his concentration to accomplish the task. Brown flings the empty vodka bottle towards the waste basket by the door. It rattles off the wall and onto the low cropped carpeted floor with a thud. This draws a glare from Charlie.

"We got his rental car…" Austin's words are slow and slurred. "At least we know that a prostitute has it…in a room he's paid for." He shifts in his squeaky bed. "Patience, it's integral to police work."

"But, five days sitting on the room and nothing." Charlie frowns. "He's not coming back, and now he's got a five day run on us."

"I told you. We'll talk to her tomorrow," Austin grunts the words as he shifts again in bed.

Charlie opens his book and skims the page for a moment before replacing his mark and closing it. He looks to his roommate. "What I don't get is why it took so long for the notice. Facial recognition at the airport had him come into the cities two months ago." Charlie's voice is pained.

Austin readjusts in his squeaky bed. "What can I tell you? It's not a perfect system. Homeland Security and the FBI…and all agencies. The technology isn't synched. It's pretty much data entry operators trying to share info. It is information overload most of the time. We can't filter fast enough."

"Yeah," Charlie's voice trails off.

Brown leans forward and checks the clock, 1:30 am. He flops down and burrows into the covers of his bed. Charlie flicks off the light on the nightstand, separates his pillows, and settles into bed. The cold, fluorescent light from the parking lot permeates the thin curtains, bathing the room in blue. "Good night," Charlie says quietly.

"Night," Austin grunts.

Chapter 7
Work Ethic

As dark as the previous night seemed, the morning light washes the gloom away with a bath of sunshine the two men need. A few blocks from their motel, Charlie and Austin sip coffee and eat breakfast at Dan's Diner. Music just at the threshold of hearing spills from above in B.W. Stevenson's "My Maria." It's floor to ceiling street-side windows allow the nourishing sunlight through as well as provide a view to the Highlander Inn. The Highlander has been their target for the last five days and the view had been pretty bland under the gloomy, gray Twin Cities skies. But today is different, a cold front has come through, pushing the clouds away, renewing their spirits. "Hey," Austin calls out. He taps the table to get Charlie's attention, checks his watch, and points across the street to the Highlander parking lot.

A woman in a short skirt, obviously a prostitute, climbs the motel stairs, a man in tow. "Busy girl," Austin quips. "It's barely 9:30 in the morning and she is working. Midwest work ethic."

Charlie cracks a smile and raises his hand to get the attention of the waitress. "Let's get over there and chat."

*   *   *

Crossing the four lanes on Cherry Avenue in the nine o'clock hour is pretty easy, there is no traffic and Charlie follows Austin, jaywalking across the street. The Highlander Inn is a cut-rate motel, advertising hourly and weekly rates. The sign itself is lettered in plaid, a rather weak affectation of the Scottish Highlands here in the Twin Cities. In the parking lot Austin scans the vehicles, finally pointing. "There's our car. Gray Ford Taurus. He's got to be around here."

The men mount the stairs with purpose. Their casual attire is perfect for the cool, but warming air. Both men wear leather jackets and jeans. Charlie is in a bomber jacket over a white t-shirt and Austin is in a black sports coat over a polo shirt. They look like law enforcement or goons coming to collect a debt, either way they are an intimidating duo.

At room 216 the men separate, planting themselves at each side of the door. "Got it?" Charlie questions.

Austin nods and raps his knuckle on the door. The door opens to a stop held by the chain. A man in a shirt and tie with his suit pants unbuckled, looks through the opening. He spies the two men and smirks. "Sorry, guys. Gonna have to wait your turn."

Austin holds up his FBI badge. "Open the fucking door." His words are those of a man who would rather pistol whip you then actually speak to you.

The ruddy-faced, balding, fifty-plus year old businessman understands that this is no time for foolishness. "Shit." His eyes drop to the floor and he fumbles with his belt.

He closes the door and unhooks the chain, reopening the door. He finishes fixing his pants and grabs at his jacket laid out on the bed. "Hey!" a voice calls out from the bathroom, followed by the prostitute in only her bra and loosened skirt. "Who are you guys?"

The business man scowls as he dons his jacket. "Cops, bitch. You set me up?"

"Shut your fucking mouth," Austin orders, slapping the man across the cheek. He points a finger at the slack-jawed lump of a human. The man holds his stinging cheek as his whole head reddens to match the handprint on his face. "How much do you owe her?"

"Nothing. I didn't get anything!" the businessman insists.

Austin begins to raise his hand again and the man flinches. Instead, Austin turns his attention to the prostitute. "What was your price?"

The prostitute puts a hand on her hip. "We agreed to $150."

"Eighty bucks. Cough it up." Austin gestures with his hand.

"I ain't paying shit!"

Austin cocks his head. "You want a trip down to the station? That'll cost you..." Austin glances at Charlie. "What? Four or five times that for solicitation, Charlie?"

Charlie purses his lips and remains silent as he nods. The man's eyes widen and he digs twenties out of his wallet. He pushes the money to Austin, who puts his hands up, backing away from the cash. "Count it out on the bed."

"Twenty, forty, sixty, eighty," the man mumbles as he counts and drops the crisp twenties.

Pocketing his wallet, the man reacts immediately to Austin's order, "Get out."

Moving to the door Austin calls out, "Wait," and the man halts.

The businessman is pale and turns and faces Austin. Brown steps forward and punches the man in the gut, folding him nearly in half, gasping for air. Charlie steps between the men, but Austin holds up his hands in surrender, halting Charlie. "That's what happens when you try to stiff a working lady out of her money. Let that be a lesson to you."

Austin shoves the man out the door as the prostitute stands by speechless, futilely trying to cover herself. Charlie shuts the door. Agent Brown's alpha-male façade drops away as he turns to the prostitute. "Sorry about that, Ms...?" He pauses, holding onto his thought a second before formally stating his question, "What's your name, Dear?"

"Jasmine," the prostitute announces quietly.

Jasmine is in her early thirties, but she is a well-worn working girl. Her strawberry hair and curvy body are still attractive enough. She yanks a loose fitting t-shirt from a bag and holds it next to her chest, partially covering her exposed milky white skin. "Jasmine," Austin pronounces the word slowly, letting it savor in his mouth. "What a pretty name." He moves forward, closing the distance as the woman backs to the wall. "Listen, we hate to bother you, but me and my partner here," Austin flashes a shy smile toward Charlie, "we have some questions to ask you. I'm with the FBI. Charlie over there, he's with the local authorities."

Austin flips open his credentials, exposing his badge. Jasmine's eyes narrow as she peers at the badge, inspecting it with skepticism. "What's this about? It can't be about the guy you just tossed out of my room."

Jasmine dons the t-shirt, revealing a printed pattern of a kitten pawing at a butterfly across the front. Austin looks her up and down, smiling at the casually dressed woman standing before him. Jasmine frowns. "What does the FBI want with me?"

"I need to know about you car," Austin states matter-of-factly.

Jasmine's frown deepens. "It's not my car."

"I've seen you drive it," Austin elaborates. "The Ford Taurus out in the parking lot, where's the guy it's rented to?"

Jasmine's bottom lip protrudes as she shrugs, "I don't know. The guy told me he had it leased for the rest of the month. He told me to take it back to the airport to Thrifty Car Rental on the last day of the month."

Austin casts a glance toward Charlie. "Am I in trouble?" Jasmine questions quietly.

Austin shakes his head, "No, no. Where'd you meet this guy?"

Jasmine hesitates. "Burnsville." She looks back and forth between Charlie and Austin. "That's where I...I do business. I asked if he wanted company outside of Club Cargo...where I conduct a lot of my business. He hired me to keep him company for three days." Jasmine smiles at the thought. "I gave him a weekly rate. A thousand bucks."

Austin continues his friendly interrogation, "Can you describe the man? Did he give you a name?"

Jasmine bites her lip. "Eli," she sighs, "I looked at the rental agreement and it said Eli Benton. As far as what he looked like..." Jasmine thinks a moment. "He was in rough shape. Skinny. Sickly. Bushy hair and beard. He had some hellacious scars across his chest. He told me they were scars from cancer surgeries."

Austin shoots a glance at Charlie before turning his attention back to Jasmine. He is about to speak, but Jasmine continues, "Eli was like a wanna-be-biker-guy, but he seemed like he was more of a yuppie."

"What makes you say that?" Austin quizzes some more.

"He bought some fancy motorcycle. Italian, maybe? He was so happy. All we did on our last day together was ride around."

Austin nods, "That's why he left the rental car with you."

"Yeah." Jasmine smiles at the thought. "He was like a little kid, and he just took off on that motorcycle."

"A Ducati?" Austin asks softly.

"That's it!" Jasmine calls out.

"Thank you." Austin bows slightly to the woman. "You've been very helpful." He turns to Charlie at the door. "Let's go, Charlie."

Outside Jasmine's room Austin smiles as, he whistles a tune and starts down the steps. "Ah, the world's oldest profession."

Charlie scowls, "What are you so happy about?"

Austin stops mid-staircase and turns to face Charlie, a couple steps above him. Charlie throws his hands in the air. "Helpful? Why would you tell her that she was helpful? How do you define helpful? Where are we going?"

Austin just grins. "What kind of detective are you? Scars and sickly equals cancer. What's here in Minnesota?"

Charlie looks to the sky as he ponders a moment. "Mayo Clinic?"

"Bingo." Austin's head slowly pivots back and forth, "We got him. He's got an appointment. We're going to Rochester."

Chapter 8
Rochester

Rochester, Minnesota

Substituting one discount motel for another, Charlie and Austin find themselves in Rochester, Minnesota, at the River View Inn. In a city known for its world-class healthcare, a large portion of the community's commerce caters to the patients and their families coming from long distances to see doctors. The hospitality sector of Rochester meets the broad spectrum of its visitors, from the five star hotels to those on a limited budget. Charlie and Austin find themselves at the lower tier of hotels. The tiny motel room is clean, albeit claustrophobic.

The accustomed positions have been assumed for the evening, Charlie in his twin bed closest to the door, Austin in the interior twin bed, nightstand between them. "Good value on this room. Fifty bucks," Austin states between sips from his pint of vodka.

The room is dark except for the television with the volume turned down. A college football game on ESPN casts shadow in different directions as the cameras rotate through various views of each play. Charlie flicks on the nightstand light and grabs his book. The clock next to the light shows 11:00 pm.

"Value?" Charlie clips the word with disgust. "You want to talk about value?" Charlie looks over at the man in the bed next to him. "Is this what you value? Every night with you now, you sucking down your *sleeping medicine*?" Charlie flips a hand at Austin and ends his sentence with finger quotes around the words "sleeping medicine."

"Who asked you?" Austin growls back.

"I'm your friend. I want you to know that I don't like it." Charlie's tone shifts into utter sarcasm, "If you're not aware, I live on a reservation where alcohol kills about a third of its citizens."

"I said, 'who asked you?'" Austin repeats the words, punctuating the question with a large swig from his bottle.

Charlie looks to the TV for a moment. He watches the running back scamper wide on a handoff, tip-toeing out of bounds. He turns his head back to Austin who is laying flat in bed, awkwardly attempting to drink from his bottle of vodka.

"I'm sorry, man. I'm just wore out," Charlie sighs. "It's hard to see you like this. Every morning we wait until you feel good enough." Charlie emphasizes the words "good enough." "What I'm trying to say is that I'm here to help you with whatever you need. We're going to get this guy, and you don't need to substitute one problem for another."

"You have no idea, Charlie," Austin's words are a whisper.

Charlie absorbs the words. He turns back to the TV and watches an attempted pass with the ball batted down at the line of scrimmage. The replays show it again and again from different angles. "I know. You are right. It's going to take time." Charlie turns back toward Austin. "You got your kids you're going to go home to."

Charlie's phone buzzes on his lap and he focuses on it, moving his glare from his drunken friend to the phone. He reads the text to himself. It is from Veronica: "All's well. Goodnight. Love you."

Charlie types out a text and replies: "Goodnight from Rochester. Be home tomorrow. I love you."

"Is that the wife?" Austin questions in a low, slow drawl influenced by the alcohol.

"Yes," Charlie replies with annoyance.

Austin takes another drink from his bottle, replaces its cap, and sets it aside. He holds up his hand and twists his wedding ring on his finger. "Everything ok back home?"

"Yup," Charlie replies. He's returned to his book. He skims the pages trying to find his spot where he last left off.

"Well, good. You'll see her tomorrow." Austin works the ring on his finger round and round. He drops his hands and feels next to him, searching for his bottle. He locates it and drinks a swallow. "I'm tired. I'm going to sleep."

"Ok," Charlie acknowledges. "Couple more pages in my book and I'll shut her down too."

"Good night," Austin mumbles.

"Night," Charlie nods the word in Austin's direction as he reads his Aldo Leopold book.

He relaxes as he reads the familiar words, finding calm in the stormy world around him. After a couple pages he marks his page and turns out the light on the nightstand. He shifts his pillows and settles into bed, positioning himself to see the football game on the wall-mounted TV.

"Charlie?" Austin calls softly.

"Yeah," Charlie replies, his tone still showing his disdain for the conversation.

"Thank you," Austin breathes the words.

"You are welcome," Charlie replies, his words are antiseptic.

"No, really. Thank you." Austin's voice is thick, "Taking all this time off. I owe you."

"Don't mention it. It's ok." Charlie shifts in his bed as he watches the game. "I have my own self interests. We are all in danger with Elliot still out there."

Austin tips the bottle to his lips as he finishes the last drops of vodka. It spills down his cheek as he attempts to drink from a prone position. He wipes at his face as the empty bottle and its cap are brushed to the floor with his other hand. "I have to tell you a story."

"Maybe you should get some sleep."

"No. No. I'm a-tell you a story," Austin's words are slurred

Charlie has met his tolerance for his drunken friend, and his tone reflects his annoyance, "Fine."

Charlie stares at the game on TV. Austin shifts in his bed curling on to his side as he closes his eyes. "Did I ever tell you my dad was a cop?" Austin questions.

"No."

"Yeah," Austin's voice rises. "He was a detective in Cleveland, where I grew up."

Chapter 9
Frank Brown

"Picture this, Charlie," Austin Brown begins his story. His words are slow and slurred. "Cleveland, Ohio in 1978. My house was gorgeous. It was in an idyllic middle class neighborhood on the edge of Cleveland City limits, just inside the limits. You had to live within the city limits to be on the force." Austin snorts a laugh at the thought of that rule. "I remember seeing the tall buildings of downtown Cleveland in the distance through the canopy of our mature deciduous trees. Big trees. Well, they seemed big to a kid. Big oak tree. A Maple. An elm. They were huge. I climbed them all. Red brick homes dominated the block with a few white, colonial houses thrown in for variety." Austin sighs, "God, Charlie, it was so nice."

Austin shifts in his bed, moving to his back. Charlie glances from the TV to the man in the bed next to him. He sees Austin, eyes closed, hands clasped behind his head. "I was eight years old when it happened. I remember it. The summer day turned to dusk and the streetlights buzzed overhead, illuminating the asphalt streets below. A police cruiser pulled into the driveway and my dad got out of the passenger side. My friend Tommy and I were just sitting on the front step and my dad yelled for Tommy to get home. He didn't have to say it twice. The tone...Tommy could hear it. He got up and sprinted home about a block away. I watched him disappear into the dusk as my dad came up the steps. He put his hand on my head...very gently."

Austin's story halts as he adjusts his pillows. "I followed my dad inside and he was hugging my mom. I heard him say that he had shot and killed somebody. He sent me to my room. I came out of my room later to use the bathroom and I could see my dad sitting at the table. His hand shook as he poured vodka from a bottle." Austin chuckles at the mention of vodka and he repeats the word with derision, "Vodka."

Austin's voice gets higher as he continues, "I had never seen my dad like this...scared I guess. It was so weird. I could hear him telling my mother that the man he killed was a terrible criminal. The perp had shot and wounded a cop earlier and it was huge manhunt that day."

Austin is out of bed. He heads to the bathroom to relieve himself. He returns to the comfort of his bed. "Where was I? Oh, yeah. My dad was tough. Frank Brown. He looked exactly like those detectives you see in the 1970's TV shows. A big guy. Six feet tall. Two hundred pounds. Mustache. Sports jacket and tie. You didn't mess with him. He was a cliché when I think about it now. My mom. She was so beautiful. Blonde. Petite. She didn't work...well, she was a homemaker. That's what they used to call stay-at-home moms."

Austin's voice is shaky as he remembers his mom. He holds back his emotions and continues as he wipes tears from his eyes. "It was the start of my dad's drinking. The beginning of the long downward spiral of my family. The long, drawn-out investigation."

Austin is on his back in bed. He covers his face with his arm, eyes buried into his elbow, but his mouth is unobstructed and he speaks freely. "My dad would get mean when he was drunk."

Charlie can hear the pain in Austin's voice. It's the first details Charlie hears of Austin's life, besides the most immediate traumatic events. The picture is becoming clearer. "It was about a week before my ninth birthday," Austin continues. "It wasn't every night, but most nights. My mom crying. My dad slapping her around. I could hear my mom's cries from my bedroom. My dad drunk and yelling at her as if she had done something wrong."

Charlie is riveted by the story. There's no sense that the alcohol is affecting Austin anymore. No words are slurred. The message of the story is coherent. Charlie realizes this is a memory Austin has relived in his head forever.

Austin continues to reveal his tale. "My mom's name was Kate. Katherine. She was so beautiful. I'll have to show you pictures sometime."

Austin takes a deep breath before he continues, contemplating the images, "Maybe I felt something in me coming on my ninth birthday, but whatever it was, it drew me out of my room for the nightly screaming. My mom was crying as usual. My dad, drunk, per usual. I was standing there in front of my dad, a little boy in flannel pajamas, pointing my finger in his face." Austin shakes his head back and forth, arm still covering his eyes. He extends his finger toward the ceiling, re-enacting the scene he describes. "It was so weird. I was looking into the eyes of a man, my dad, but his eyes made it seem like he was dead inside. My dad didn't seem strong. As I think about it now, he was sickly. Thin."

Austin is up from the bed getting a bottle of water. He cracks it open and drinks. The light of the TV is enough for him to accomplish the task unimpeded, and Charlie watches in silence. Austin never gives a look in Charlie's direction. He just crawls into bed and picks up where he left off. His eyes closed again, he resumes the story. "This is about a year after the shooting. My dad still hadn't been cleared. After a year! The assailant that had shot the cop earlier, he was black, and my dad shot him in self defense. Multiple witnesses heard the black guy say he wasn't coming in alive. I saw the story on the news. You have to remember that this was the seventies; the racial component was raging in every segment of society. Black Panthers protested. Jesse Jackson. Al Sharpton. They burned two blocks of the city. Not the good part of the city, mind you, the black neighborhoods. Can you imagine?"

Austin laughs at the thought. "I guess a lot of stuff is still the same. But anyway, there I was a little kid; I remember it plain as day. I stood in front of my dad in a calm voice and told him if he didn't stop hurting mom, I would kill him. He just laughed at me like a mad man. He had a half a glass of whiskey in his hand and he downed it in a gulp, punctuating the act by smashing the glass so hard onto the table, it cracked the glass. It cut his hand. Did I tell you already that my dad was sickly by then? Skinny, skinny. He never ate anything...that I saw anyway. He drank all the time he was home. He was on restricted duty at the precinct sitting around doing nothing. Watching the Black Panthers picket the police station. I remember him complaining about that and seeing it on the local TV stations."

Charlie is mesmerized by the story. It is a tale he is familiar with. Alcohol on the reservation, tearing families apart. He holds his tongue, waiting for Austin to continue and he does, "Thank God for my mom. The broken glass and cut hand enraged my father. Enraged! My mom darted between me and my dad shuffling me to my room before tending to my father's hand." Austin lets loose a laugh. "I'm lucky she got between us. I might not even be here."

Austin drinks from his water bottle, eyes never opening. "Flash forward two years. I turned eleven years old and this was still going on, intermittently mind you, but at least once a month there would be drunken chaos. He full-on alcoholic. There were some not-so-rocky times though. My dad and I spent time together. I was in the scouts and he took me out camping. Even showed me how to shoot his pistol. I could shoot it pretty good. He had some almost-sober weeks here and there."

Charlie can hear the pain inflection rise back into Austin's voice, "My dad was finally cleared of any wrong-doing in the shooting, but the damage was done. It was too late. Alcohol gripped his life completely. Drunk every night."

Charlie can hear Austin's voice waver now as he continues, "It was a particularly bad evening. The battle was raging, not the yelling so much as the smack of the back of his hand. Same pattern we see now, Charlie. Woman won't leave. Doesn't know how to get away safely. Women got more resources now, but we still see it."

"Anyway," Austin pauses, drawing a deep breath. "Dad was beating up Mom again. I went to my parents' room. There was my dad's jacket on the back of the chair as always, and as always, there was his shoulder holster and pistol. I took the pistol and headed to the living room. I could hear the gasping in the hallway, a sound I had never heard before."

Austin's voice has a cry in it. He wipes at tears squeezing from his closed eyes as he continues. "It was too much for me. Three years. I moved into the kitchen area and my father was on top of my mother, hands clenched around her neck. She was gasping, dying. Her trachea had been crushed. It was too late. My father turned to me; he half-heartedly tried to stop me. He was almost smiling it seemed. I swear after all this time...I think he was proud of me...for standing up to him."

Austin sobs softly, "I couldn't save her Charlie. I pulled the trigger three years too late. I killed my father that night, literally, with a bullet to the head, and my mother figuratively. I had gotten the courage, but it was too late."

Charlie listens to the man cry. He can see Austin drink from the water bottle and toss it aside. Austin heaves a shuddering sob. "I told him I would kill him, and I did." He repositions himself on his side facing away from Charlie and snorts a laugh. It sounds like a drunken laugh suddenly to Charlie. "Look at me now. Like father, like son. Drunk."

Austin heaves a sign, his voice is almost a whisper, "I'm going to kill that man."

In just a few seconds, Charlie hears the steady breathing of a man asleep. He wipes at his eyes freeing his own tears of emotion. He adjusts himself in bed, rolling onto his back. He holds up his left hand and stares at the wedding ring on his hand. He twists it with his other hand a moment before noticing the water stain on the ceiling tiles above. He drops his hands to his side and buries them under the covers. He closes his eyes and then opens them, fixing his view on the stain, and straining to see in the light from the TV. "It looks like a squid," he whispers to himself. He reaches for the remote control on the nightstand and clicks off the TV.

Chapter 10
Mayo Clinic

The Mayo Clinic's hospital campus area reflects its reputation as a world renowned medical facility; it is large and modern, sporting the latest architecture. Charlie and Austin notice the unique and unusual design of the Nurses' Island as they approach the counter. The nurses' station and waiting area are brightly lit by the second-story skylights and elevated ceiling that some might call a waste of space, but it is beautiful and the centerpiece of the room over the nurses' station, an octagonal shaped, waist high counter with one side open for easy entrance and egress by the nurses. Soft, soothing, familiar, instrumental music in the form of Floyd Cramer's "Last Date" spills around waiting patients from hidden speakers. Austin steps to the counter and grasps the edge of the counter with both hands. He is all business while Charlie is mesmerized, his eyes scanning the luxury-hotel-lobby-esque building. He stands behind Austin, smiling at the nurse. His eyes still continue to move, taking in his surroundings, darting to the skylights and patients in the waiting area. The nurse sits on an ergonomic chair in front of her computer. "May I help you?" she inquires with only a hint of a smile.

She is an attractive woman with noticeably large diamonds on her finger and in each ear lobe. Charlie can't help notice her hair pulled back in a ponytail exposing her ear lobes and thinking to himself the lack of a diamond ring for his wife. Her name tag reads "Monica" and Austin emphasizes her name as he pulls his credentials from his sports jacket pocket. "Monica, yes you may help me. I'm FBI Special Agent Austin Brown and this is my associate, Sergeant Charlie LeBeau."

Charlie leans around Austin to make eye contact with the woman. He waves, "Nice place you got here."

"Thank you," Monica replies, her smile increases ever-so-slightly.

Austin pockets his badge. "I'd like some information on a patient. Likely a cancer patient. His name is Elliot Kauffman, but he may be under an alias. You might also look under Eli Benton."

The nurse's answer is polished from receiving this routine question many times. "I'm sorry. Unless you have a warrant, I can't release any medical information on any patient."

Austin reaches for his FBI credentials and extends them again toward the woman. "You can't make an exception? We're talking about a known murderer here."

The nurse shakes her head. "Doctor-patient confidentiality."

Charlie is still taking in the large atrium that includes the waiting room. The skylights glow as they allow the sunshine to spill inside, illuminating many live plants. Charlie notes to himself that this is a far cry from the sterile, gray medical facilities he's accustomed. His peaceful thoughts are interrupted as he flinches to the crash of Austin's fist slamming down on the counter. The large room is silenced as all eyes are suddenly on Austin. Charlie steps forward and grabs an angry Austin by both of his arms. The FBI agent glares at the nurse. He grits his teeth, but remains silent and is compliant with Charlie as his friend leads him away from the counter. Charlie provides an uncomfortable grin and apology to the nurse, "I'm sorry. It's been a long couple days."

Charlie eases Austin down the hallway toward the exit, still holding the sleeve of his jacket. "Let's go."

After a few steps, Austin wrenches his arm from Charlie's grip. "I'm not a child."

Charlie halts, letting Austin get some distance, before resuming his pace. "What did you expect?" Charlie calls ahead to his friend. "She was just doing her job."

"Let's just go home," Austin mumbles over his shoulder. He buries his hands in his pockets and bows his head, looking down at his feet as he walks.

Chapter 11
Patience

Rural Minnesota

Charlie has the first driving shift as he sits behind the wheel of Austin's Chevy Malibu heading west on U.S. Highway 14. Austin is in the passenger seat, eyes closed, head resting against the window. Charlie listens to a series of songs on the country music radio station that includes: "I Got the Hoss" by Mel Tillis, "Stay Gone" by Jimmy Wayne, and Waylon Jennings with his song "Luckenbach, Texas." The bright sunshine has given way to high thin clouds, dampening the late morning mood. "Dead end," Austin mumbles with his eyes closed, his first words in the half-hour since leaving the hospital. Keith Whitley sings on the radio, "I'm Over You."

"Do you mind if we tune the radio to something a little more cheery than this?" Austin questions, still holding his eyes shut.

Charlie pushes the seek button and the radio tunes in "Saturday Night" by the Bay City Rollers, and Austin nods approvingly to the beat. Out of the urban area and into the countryside, the car follows Highway 14 winding through the adjacent fields of corn and soybeans. Every ten miles or so they slow and pass through a small farm town. Rural Minnesota is in full harvest mode. The fields are drying and revealing their tans and browns of fall. "Did you hear me?" Austin questions, eyes still closed. "I said, 'dead end.'"

Charlie responds to his friend, "Patience. Rome wasn't built in a day."

"He'd been there," Austin mumbles, eyes still closed. "I could feel it."

"We'll get 'im, "Charlie confidently says the words. "Patience. He doesn't know that we know he's sick...or that we know anything." Charlie looks over at his listless passenger. "You think he's dying and that's why there's been this sudden reappearance? His last hurrah?"

The question gets a minimal reaction from Austin, "Yup. No doubt he's trying to take down as many of us as he can. Starting with those that exposed him."

"Blaze of glory, huh?"

Austin purses his lips. "I wouldn't call it that. I'm going to make sure it is a fizzling whimper when I get my hands on him."

"What do we do now?"

Austin's head lolls against the window, moving with the sway of the car. He folds his arms and settles deeper into his seat, eyes still closed. "I'm going to call in some favors. See if I can get his medical records through the Twin Cities FBI office. I think we can track him through any drugs he might be prescribed. I'm sure they'll share that information with me."

Charlie frowns. "Ah, it always leads back to drugs in the crime world."

Austin manages a weak smile as he relaxes. He blindly reaches for the vent and redirects the air toward the window and his face. "So, you're married now? Thanks for the invite to the wedding."

Charlie steals a glance at his passenger, happy in the change of conversation. "I'm sorry. It was an emergency wedding. I wanted Veronica to move in so we would have her protected. I just thought it'd be easier to put up with the gossip if we were married and living together. Lord knows the hell I've already caught for marrying a white girl."

Austin grins at the comment. "I suspect he'll make a run at her. At me. At you. If I have anything to say about it, we'll get him first. The best defense is a good offense."

Charlie maneuvers around a big, green, John Deere combine heading to another cornfield. The swerve bounces Austin's head against the glass. "Sorry about that," Charlie chuckles.

Austin doesn't even open his eyes. "You got Skip and Jeremy on the watch, looking out for Veronica?"

"Yeah."

"How about a gun?" Austin inquires. "Did you give her a weapon and show her how to use it?"

"Yeah," Charlie meekly answers. "She's not confident though. She can shoot. Reload. Basics. But, she is real tentative."

"What about Claude?" Austin questions. "He's got the biggest target on his back out of anyone. He frickin' shot Elliot."

"No argument there. Claude is definitely on high alert. He can take care of himself. He told me he'd used his pistol in Vietnam in close quarters. I don't worry about him. Nat and Veronica, they're my worries."

Austin's voice is relaxed. He maintains his resting demeanor. "She'll be fine. They'll be fine. I'm gonna take care of this once and for all."

Charlie steals glances at his partner as they drive in silence for a couple miles. "I wanna tell you something, but you got to swear to me that you'll keep it to yourself."

Austin's head bobbles against the window over some marginal pavement. His voice his filled with vibrato due to the highway's rough patch. "You have my word."

Charlie's voice is almost a laugh. "Veronica's going to be more than fine…we…had to get married…"

Austin's eyes flick open and he turns his head as he straightens in his seat. He grins wildly. "You old devil, you. Charlie LeBeau. I didn't know you had it in ya. I should have known it wasn't marriage just for airs."

Charlie holds a finger to his lips. "Nobody knows. Only you, me, Veronica, and her doctor. That's it. You can't say anything. Everyone thinks we got married so she could move in with me and be more, you know, comfortable in the small town gossip. But, she's…"

"With child," Austin finishes Charlie's sentence. He beams.

"Claude and Nat don't even know." Charlie holds up a finger of warning. "Please keep this to yourself."

"What?" Austin chuckles. "I can keep a secret!"

Charlie looks at his friend, "It's nice to see you smile. I haven't seen that since…"

Austin's smile morphs into a different expression, becoming more of a pained look. "I know, Charlie. It's like a bad dream…I just can't wake up."

A couple miles go by in silence. The clouds thicken and the autumn day becomes more typical of the changing, unpredictable seasonal weather. It threatens a cold rain. "You headin' back to Pierre?" Charlie finally breaks the silence.

"I guess." Austin looks out his window. "No reason to though. Kids are out in Indiana with their grandma."

"I was just thinkin'. You could stay in Sisseton," Charlie's words trail off, unsure how they might be received. "We could put you up at Veronica's house for as long as you like. What do you think? It's just sittin' there empty."

Austin looks down the highway a few moments, thinking. His head slowly begins to nod with the slightest affirmation. He whispers the words, "I'll do it."

Charlie is all smiles. "Yes! Good. Let me call Veronica when we stop and get gas up here and let her know."

Charlie points out the windshield. A harvested cornfield is circled by ducks. The cloud of ducks dips and dives forming ever-changing shapes. "Check it out!"

Austin follows Charlie's finger. "Cool. It looks like a tornado."

"Cold weather up north," Charlie states. "I heard on the weather that they're getting some snow along the Canadian border and temps in the single digits in North Dakota. That'll push the mallards down."

Charlie looks to his passenger. "You interested in getting a license and going duck hunting with us?"

Austin frowns. He shrugs with ambivalence. "Maybe."

"Good. That's a yes to me!" Charlie chirps. "It'll be fun. You never been?" Austin shakes his head. "We'll definitely do it then!"

"Lido" by Boz Scaggs fills the interior of the car as Charlie turns up the volume on the radio.

Chapter 12
Home Security

Sisseton, South Dakota

A couple miles west of Sisseton's City limits, Charlie's manufactured home sits on two acres. His homestead allotment was awarded to him by the Tribe per his request. It was always his dream to put a claim on this acreage. This is where he learned to hunt deer at the feet of his dad. He had fulfilled that dream ten years ago with a petition to the Tribal Council, and had his very own home on his property a year later.

Sisseton, South Dakota, is a sort of defacto capitol of the Sisseton-Wahpeton Sioux Tribe. There is not a capitol, per se, of the Indian Reservation; the Tribal Headquarters is located in the small community just a few miles south of Sisseton called Agency Village. Sisseton is the hub of the reservation, the center of commerce in the area. With a population of approximately 2,500 people, it hosts a mix of Indian and non-Indian citizens. Located in northeast South Dakota, the Sisseton-Wahpeton Reservation enjoys the protection of its rural location. The biggest city in the area is probably considered Fargo, North Dakota, about 90 miles to the north. Sisseton is the county seat for Roberts County and a good portion of the townsfolk cater to those areas of public service. Interstate 29 is on the east end of town and connects to Fargo to the north and Sioux Falls to the south.

Charlie's house is along the base of the Coteau Des Prairie, "the slope in the prairie." This unique geological formation with the French moniker is one of those strange occurrences in nature. The product of glaciers ten thousand years ago, it avoided and survived the leveling forces of the sheets of ice. The slope rises up west of Sisseton at about at about a 3% grade over a mile and a half. Its peak elevation then flattens into rolling hills as you travel west about twenty five miles before it drops down again, reducing elevation of about 500 feet over five miles. The western edge of the Coteau drops down to the level ground of the James River Valley, premium tillable ground perfectly suited for farming. The Coteau Des Prairies is like a three dimensional trapezoid with a wide base and narrow, flat top stretching about 100 miles long from the northwest to southeast. It juts just into the southern border of North Dakota and extends southward to about Watertown, South Dakota. The reservation boundary basically encompasses the Coteau Des Prairies.

The slopes of the trapezoid are covered with stands of trees, mostly oaks. The top of the Coteau is rocky, clay-heavy soil, less suited for farming, more in line with prairie grass and grazing. It is dotted with lakes, sloughs, and ponds. It is a hunting and fishing paradise.

Charlie's house is at the bottom of the eastern slope. A coulee, or drainage area, runs just a few dozen yards from his house and is home to wildlife that includes an abundance of deer, turkey, raccoons, and an occasional bobcat. Charlie pulls the car into his driveway and the men exit the vehicle. Stretching, Austin observes the scenery. "Man, I can't get over how awesome your house is. I love this location. Every direction...it's beautiful."

Austin looks to the east towards Minnesota, from whence they just came. The visibility is limited with the overcast sky, but you can see the flat farmland extending ever eastward. In the other directions, beyond the trees, north and south you can see the combination of the Coteau and the flatlands. Directly to the west you can look up and see the top of the slope a couple miles away. The hillsides are streaked with trees that fill the drainages. Charlie acknowledges the compliment, "Thanks. Let me run in and get the key for Veronica's. We'll head over and get you settled in."

Charlie bounds up the steps to the front deck. He stops. "You wanna come in and say 'hi' to my dad?"

Austin waves away the question, "Nah, let's just go." He continues to study the view, absorbing the autumnal surroundings.

Charlie steps through the front door into the living room. The living room is dominated by the sixty-inch flat screen TV and a beautiful whitetail buck shoulder mount hanging on the wall seemingly vigilant in its duty of watching the front entrance. The deer, taken just a half mile from the house, has a near perfect rack of antlers. Heavy, symmetrical, and wide, it is the only deer Charlie has ever considered worthy of taxidermy in his 30-plus years of hunting. Many other fine bucks have fallen to his rifle, but this deer is the once-in-a lifetime deer, and Charlie honors it as such. It's a ritual tribute for Charlie to make eye contact with the deer on the wall upon returning home and acknowledge his blessings in his life.

Inside his modest home, Charlie finds his father, Claude lounging in a recliner, reading a magazine with the television on and volume low. Claude is a graying, older version of Charlie. His hair is thinning a little, and the white hair contrasts against his dark skin. "Hey, Dad. What are you doing here? I thought I asked you to keep an eye on Veronica."

Claude peers at his son over his reading glasses. "Bah, I drop her off and pick her up. In broad daylight nothing's gonna happen. Besides, she's got a new girl now. She's got help from that intern program from North Dakota State. Kammi, Kelli, or something."

"That's right. I forgot about her new intern." Charlie hauls his suitcase to his bedroom at the far side of the house. Charlie's house is laid out with the front door opening into the living room. To the right are two bedrooms and a bathroom, this is Nat's and Claude's side of the house. To the left, through the living room and past the kitchen-dining area is the master suite.

In his bedroom, Charlie briefly stops to check on the pistol stowed in the nightstand next to the bed. He opens the revolver and inspects the bullets in all but one of the chambers. He cocks the pistol and then eases the hammer down on the empty chamber. From the living room Claude calls to him, "And you? You're back. Did you get 'im?"

Charlie returns the pistol to the drawer and moves back into the kitchen-dining area. "No such luck. I'm just here to get the keys for Veronica's place. Agent Brown's gonna crash there while we regroup."

Charlie pulls a key from a rack hanging on the wall. He circles back to the living room into his dad's line of sight. "You got your weapon ready?"

Claude looks up from his magazine, on the verge of annoyance. "It's in the bedroom. Don't be so paranoid. This guy comes after us, we'll get 'im. I already shot him once. I know what I'm doing."

Charlie is satisfied with the answer. "Can't be too careful. Alright, we'll see you later."

Claude closes his magazine and folds the recliner down. He stands with effort and moves to the window. "I'm a belt and suspenders type of guy. I got the pistol in the bedroom. Deer rifle in the closet and the shotgun in the pantry. Believe me, anybody comes in here uninvited, they're in for a surprise." He peers through a space in the curtain, avoiding moving the drapes and drawing attention. Outside, Agent Brown leans against his Malibu, arms folded, staring into the distance. "How's your friend?"

Charlie frowns and clucks his tongue. "Less than great. Puts himself to sleep with a bottle every night. Frankly, I'm a little concerned."

"You say something to him?" Claude questions.

"Yeah." Charlie is somewhat offended by the question.

"Can't help him if he doesn't want help." Claude looks to Charlie. "Maybe he'll never get over it."

"Maybe." Charlie slaps the key in his hands. "I gotta go get Veronica. We'll see you later."

Down the steps and toward his old Ford pickup, Charlie walks with a purpose. He holds up the keys. "I got 'em. Let's go. Follow me."

Austin eases behind the wheel of his Malibu. He backs the vehicle out of the way to let Charlie pass. Charlie fires up his truck and pulls next to the Malibu rolling down his window. "I'm going to pick up Veronica at the newspaper office. Most of her stuff is still there, so it's fully furnished, but she can show you everything. If you still need something, you can run out to Alco and pretty much find whatever you might need."

Austin puts his car in gear. "10-4. Lead the way."

Chapter 13
Sisters

Central Business District – Sisseton, South Dakota

The Roberts County Standard newspaper office resides in a modern steel building on First Avenue in the central business district of Sisseton. It's less than a ten minute drive from Charlie's to the newspaper office and he parks his truck on the street in front of the building. The large glass store-front windows facing the street not necessary for a newspaper office, but in the building's previous iterations as craft shop, cup cake store, and other main street-type businesses, the windows assisted sales by displaying the wares. Now the floor-to-ceiling glass store front just provides a beautifully lit workspace.

Charlie enters the newspaper office to the gong of the door indicator. "Hi, Honey! I'm home!"

"We're back here!" Veronica's voice calls out from behind stacks of boxes.

Veronica Lewis-LeBeau just turned thirty seven years old. She is a beautiful brunette with shoulder length hair that frames her pretty face perfectly, along the lines of Jennifer Anniston in her prime. Charlie's heart still skips a beat every time he sees her.

"Hi, Charlie." Veronica steps clear of the desk and boxes and gives her husband a big welcoming hug. She releases her man and gestures to the young lady smiling next to her. "I'd like to introduce my new reporter and all-around helper. This is Kelli Burnbaugh. North Dakota State University hooked me up with her through their journalism intern program. I got her the whole semester!"

Kelli is a bubbly, brunette. She is a shade shorter than Veronica and a bit on the thin side. She extends her hand and Charlie shakes it. "Nice to meet you. I've been hearing all about you."

"Likewise...on the nice to meet you part. I haven't heard about you at all." Charlie takes a step back and looks the women up and down. "Jeez, you two could be sisters."

"Oh, stop." Veronica slaps Charlie on the shoulder.

"You're not the first one to say that," Kelli pipes up. "Remember at the store, checking out. The clerk that knew you, she asked if I was your sister."

Veronica shrugs as Charlie continues, "Either way, man, we're getting some pretty girls in this town."

The women blush demurely with a giggle. "I told you he's a smooth talker," Veronica faux whispers, loud enough for Charlie to hear.

The radio in the back of the office interrupts conversation a moment as the DJ speaks, "That was one of my all time favorites here on Pheasant Country, 'When We Get Behind Closed Doors' By Charlie Rich. Now it's Eddie Rabbit with 'Hearts on Fire."

The music plays and Charlie reaches for Veronica's hand, making eye contact with Kelli. "You'll have to excuse me, but I have to steal your boss away for a few minutes."

Veronica follows Charlie toward the door. "You're in charge," she calls over her shoulder to Kelli.

Out on the street by his truck, Charlie pulls Veronica close for a kiss. "I missed you," she whispers.

"Same here," Charlie replies, wrapping his arms around the petite woman. "Everything ok with...you know?"

"Yup."

Charlie kisses her on the lips. The hum of Austin's window rolling down is followed by the Agent sticking his head out the window prodding the situation along. "Ok, lovebirds, sometime today, please."

Charlie laughs. "Look, I brought along a wet blanket."

Veronica waves. "Hi, Austin. Come on, follow us."

Chapter 14
The Un-Official

Just a few blocks from the newspaper office on 8th Avenue West, Veronica's house sits across from the high school. Charlie pulls into the driveway and Austin parks on the street. The house is a 1960's construction, single story with basement. Towering, mature trees, with most of their leaves dropped and covering the lawn, envelop the yard.

All three gather in the driveway. Veronica hugs Austin. "You doing ok?"

Austin nods and the Veronica tour begins, "High School right over there. One car garage." She pauses and sidles up to Charlie. "Any news?"

Charlie grimaces. "Nope. Pretty sure he's dying. Can't confirm confidential medical stuff, you know. They wanted warrants."

"Well, I'm glad you called me when you did." Veronica steps toward the front door of the house. "I was just about to tell Kelli she could stay here."

"Oh, no." Charlie's brow furrows. Where's she going to stay?"

"No, no," Veronica quickly rebuts. "She's been staying with her aunt. Up by the hospital."

"Ok, good."

Veronica smiles and steps up on the front porch with the key. "Hey, Austin, all these leaves can be raked up. Maybe earn your rent." Veronica giggles.

"Sure," Austin replies with a shrug. "Nothing like a little manual labor to get my mind off things."

Veronica turns her attention from the door lock to Charlie, then to Austin. Her expression is filled with concern. "I was just kidding."

"I'm not. I'd be glad to do it." Austin's stone-faced expression gives nothing away.

Veronica rolls her eyes, giving a nod to Charlie as she unlocks the front door. "Come on in. I'll show you around."

They tour the house and Veronica points out the three bedrooms and one bathroom. The house is tidy and minimally decorated. "Carpet's a little worn," Veronica points out. "Clean sheets and towels are in this closet. More towels under the sink. Got a washer and dryer in the laundry room just off the garage. You probably got some clothes to wash."

Austin nods. "So," Veronica's hands bounce off her sides. "What's your guys' next move? Am I safe?" The group moves into the living room and Veronica opens the curtains, exposing the nice picture window with a view of the high school and the Coteau behind it.

Charlie moves to Veronica and puts his arm around her. "I got you."

"Seriously," Veronica's voice is more demanding. "How bad is it?"

Charlie looks to Austin, "It's kind of a dead end at the moment."

Austin's head bobs and weaves as he begins to speak, "I'm working some favors. He's dying, as Charlie said. Well, that's our hypothesis anyway...Mayo Clinic and all. I'm guessing he's getting some meds. Painkillers probably. I got FBI connections that I already called on. They're digging for me."

"I don't understand," Veronica's tone is one of annoyance. "Why isn't the FBI out there in full force? One of their own is gone, and it seems like they don't care."

"It's not that simple." Austin folds his arms and leans against the wall. "They busted ass for two weeks. All hands on deck. Now they're back to the business model of the day...counter-terrorism. I'm what the FBI has on the case...I'm an un-official. A Hessian soldier to do some dirty work."

"What?" Veronica's face crinkles with her question. "I don't understand. Can't you just get warrants and some agents to get Elliot?"

"If only it were so simple. The FBI's mission is the war on terror. There's not much of a cry for a federal investigation of local murders. Murder on the reservation is not viewed as a national emergency. To quote my boss, 'Let the locals handle local crime.' So, right now, if it isn't radical Islam terrorism, the FBI leaves it to the local authorities."

"Seriously?" Veronica questions again. "An agent's family member is harmed, and the FBI won't intervene?"

Austin frowns and shakes his head, "The FBI's effort is me. They've given me the latitude to handle this business, which is a pretty sweet deal actually."

"I'm two months into six months of administrative leave. I was ordered to stay away from the case with a wink and a nod."

"Whoa," Veronica breathes the word.

Austin continues his matter-of-fact recounting of his status. "Everyone up the chain of command has plausible deniability. I only tell you this because I'll deny it too, if something goes wrong. I'm technically on a combination of family medical leave and grief admin leave for 'mental health.' Still getting my full pay." Austin shrugs and a half-hearted smile creases his lips. "It's just me and your hubby on the case."

"So, where does that leave me? Us?" Veronica interlocks her fingers with Charlie.

"Same old," Austin pronounces the words slowly.

Veronica shakes her head. "I've been thinking about this...a lot. I figure I'm some kind of bait. I'm going to lure him in and you'll get him."

"I didn't want to say anything…" Austin's words trail off and he finishes the thought with a nod. Veronica flinches at the gesture. "There's also, Claude," Austin picks up the conversation. "Charlie and I were just talking about Claude having put a bullet in Elliot…"

Austin pauses as he sees Veronica cringe again and give him a glare.

Charlie holds up a hand, interjecting, "Um, that name is not spoken aloud."

"Oh, gotcha," Austin's head goes back in understanding. "Anyhoo, Claude is as much of a target as anyone."

"We are not in bad shape," Charlie speaks softly, comfortingly. "We are on our home turf. This is a small town. Word's out. We got eyes everywhere looking for strangers."

Silence grips the group for a few moments before Veronica speaks, "Are you ok, Austin? This is all still so overwhelming. How are you holding up?"

"I'm not going to lie to you. I'm not good, but probably as best as could be expected given the circumstances. I know my kids are safe with their grandparents, and I only have one mission in life, and I won't rest until Elliot's dead."

Veronica recoils at the name. Austin grimaces, "Sorry, I forgot. I'm serious. I'm going to kill that man. I've already sworn that to your husband…by the way congrats and congrats."

"Thank…" Veronica's cuts herself off, eyes widening, she shoves Charlie. "What did you tell him? Did you tell him?" Charlie cowers as he tries to cushion the slaps to his shoulder. "You told him? You told him? Oh, I'm so embarrassed." Veronica covers her face with her hands as she looks at the floor.

Austin is amused and Charlie enjoys the moment. A temporary reprieve for his friend. Definitely worth it for him. "Relax," Austin growls. "He swore me to secrecy. You're baby-bump is safe with me. Besides, who the hell am I going to tell anyway?" His hands flail at his sides.

Veronica peeks through her fingers at the smiling FBI man. She can't help but laugh. "Fine," she concedes.

"But, seriously," the joy is out of Agent Brown's voice. "I'm going to kill that man."

Veronica laughs uncomfortably at Agent Brown's matter-of-fact statement.

"You going back to work tomorrow, Charlie?" Austin changes the subject.

"Yeah, but Skip knows I might have to leave at the drop of a hat."

Austin sighs. "Thanks again for the use of the house."

"Sure, you're more than welcome." Veronica hands over the key. "You're welcome to stay as long as you need to."

"Speaking of being welcome," Charlie chimes in, "you're more than welcome to come to supper. I'm sure Claude's got something cooking."

Veronica smiles. "I think he said scalloped potatoes and ham tonight."

"Knowing Claude, I'm sure he calls it 'scalped' potatoes and ham." Charlie rolls his eyes.

Veronica snorts a laugh. " You're right!"

"Thanks, but I'm just gonna chill tonight." Austin pushes himself from the wall. He points a finger first at Veronica then indicates with his thumb. "Your hubby and me...we've probably had enough of each other. Could use a break I'm sure."

"I'm not that easy to ditch." Charlie holds up his hand. "I'll bring you a plate later. Couple things I want to discuss with you."

Austin's shoulders bounce with a contained laugh. "Sure. No sense in tryin' to argue."

Chapter 15
Lookout

Charlie and Veronica load up in Charlie's truck, getting out of the way for Austin to settle into the house. With a wave they back out of the driveway as Austin waits to back his car into the driveway and unload his suitcase.

The five block drive from Veronica's house back to the newspaper office is made in silence. Parked outside of the newspaper office, Veronica unbuckles her seat belt and leans over to kiss Charlie goodbye. She kisses him, but as she pulls away, Charlie grabs her arm and turns the rumbling engine off. "Listen, I have to tell you about Austin. He's drunk every night. I wouldn't be surprised right now if he's at the liquor store. That's why I wanted to bring him a plate of food tonight, to check on him. I'm kinda worried."

Veronica's mouth twists into a frown. "I didn't say anything, but he doesn't look good. His complexion is gray. He's lost weight. And what was that statement about killing you-know-who?"

"Oh, my God." Charlie pushes himself back into bench seat of his truck. "I thought growing up on the reservation was tough. Agent Brown's childhood. Now that was something. His father was a cop, an alcoholic cop. Austin shot his dad dead when he was eleven years old. His father had killed his mother."

"What? My God!" Veronica shouts the words.

"It's messed up, man." Charlie shakes his head, still amazed by the information he is sharing. Charlie leans over and kisses Veronica. "I'm gonna go. I'll fill you in on the details tonight. Call me when you want to come home. One of us will come get you."

Veronica slides out the door. "Ok. Bye."

Chapter 16
Arm Chair Scout

Back at Charlie's house, Claude is reclined in his chair dozing when Charlie returns home. He wakes with a start as Charlie opens the door. "Who's there?" Claude calls out.

"Just me, Dad," Charlie sighs. "That looks comfortable. I could use a nap. I'm beat."

Claude sits up in his chair, pushing the lever on the recliner and lowering his feet to the floor. "I got something that will recharge your batteries. Just found out the ducks are pouring in from up north. Must be a cold front pushin' em."

"Really?" Charlie questions. "I saw a few over in Minnesota on the way back today. I heard on the radio that they're getting winter weather on the Canadian border."

Charlie flops down on the couch and Claude continues, "Cold front must be dippin' further south than that. I bumped into Ol' Kyle Hanahan, foreman up there on the Bishop Ranch. He said Dumarce Lake was so full of mallards you couldn't see water."

Charlie scoffs, "I don't know 'bout that. Dumarce is pretty big."

"You know Kyle." Claude holds his thumb and fore finger close together. "He's a bit prone to exaggeration."

"What do you think? Should we head up there this weekend?"

"I'm up for it. Sooner the better. Be nice to put some fresh mallards on the table and in the freezer."

Charlie closes his eyes and settles into the cushy couch. "I can't just take off. I've been gone ten days. Skip's expecting me back tomorrow. It's gonna have to wait until Saturday."

"I hear ya."

"Is Nat around this weekend?" Charlie questions.

"Yeah, I already talked to him, and he's in. Veronica said it was ok, if you're wondering about that."

Charlie turns his head toward his dad and strains to open one eye. He grins, "Yup, I guess I need permission for everything now." He closes his eyes and relaxes again.

Claude rubs his chin and yawns. "Veronica said she's never had duck, so she's looking forward to it."

"Sounds like we're committed to the plan then," Charlie mumbles.

"It sure is nice to have a woman in the house. I don't know how we were gettin' by before." Charlie opens one eye and glances at his father a moment before closing it again. "Yup, she really took good care of us while you were gone. And she can cook! Another chef in the rotation, less work for me."

"Glad you've adjusted already," Charlie chimes in.

"That girl is sophisticated and smart. I think our conversation around the supper table went up by twenty-five IQ points...of course now you're back, it'll probably trend down a bit."

"Ha. Ha," Charlie emits a dispassionate, forced laugh.

Claude is on a roll. "Seriously though, what kind of honeymoon did you newlyweds have? You get married, then go off for ten days with Agent Brown. Highly questionable in my book."

"I'm not going to dignify that with a response."

"I figured you wouldn't."

Claude relaxes back into his recliner and rocks in the chair as the silence settles in the room, disturbed only by the squeak of the chair gliding back and forth. Charlie's eyes remain closed as he asks, "What do you think about Agent Brown coming with to shoot some ducks? Talk about a guy going through hell. He could really use a distraction to get his mind off things."

Claude shrugs indifferently. "Sure. The more, the merrier...and another limit of ducks to fill."

"I'm going to ask him." Charlie breathes deeply. "Hey, what about the Hakken's cornfields right by the house? Any ducks around here yet?"

"Nada." Claude frowns.

"They'll be in here soon enough. Pete and Lars won't mind if we hunt. I'll give 'em a call to let 'em know."

Claude looks to the ceiling, imagining a moment as his expression reflects youthful joy. "Nothing better than hearing that rush of wings when mallards are circlin' a cornfield. I can't wait."

"Keep an eye out, "Charlie orders. "Those ducks come in, I'll definitely burn a couple hours of leave if I have to."

Chapter 17
Highball

The long day moves to night for Charlie. After being on the road for ten days and traveling back from Rochester this afternoon, he's ready for bed at 8 pm, but it's not to be. Charlie is welcomed at the front door of Veronica's house by Agent Brown, amber glass of liquid in hand. Austin's big smile greets Charlie and he invites him inside. "Come on in!" Austin boisterously shouts the order.

"I see you're settling in. You found the highball glasses." Charlie steps inside. "I brought you some food, as promised."

"You didn't have to do that," Austin retorts.

Charlie moves to the dining room. He spies the opened Crown Royal box on the empty table, its purple bag crumpled next to the box. The bottle is a quarter gone, as it rests on the counter next to the fridge and a half-full ice tray. "Did you eat?" Charlie questions.

Agent Brown holds up his glass. "Not yet. Just enjoying a cocktail. You want one?"

"So, how we doing tonight?" Charlie's tone is annoyed.

Agent Brown is unphased. He is feeling no pain. "Good. I'm treating myself to some good stuff. Just thought I'd celebrate your guys' kindness on letting me stay here. Thank you so much by the way." He sips from his glass.

"You are very welcome, and no thank you on the drink." Charlie sets the heavily weighted, foil covered plate on the dining room table. "It's scalloped potatoes and ham, like Veronica said. Claude said three minutes on medium heat in the microwave should warm it up good."

"You guys are too much." Austin grimaces as he sips from his glass. "You didn't have to do that."

"Well, I kinda feel I have to." Charlie points to the dining room table and chairs. "Can we sit and talk?"

"Sure," Austin shrugs. He springs into action clearing the table of the box and bag. "I'm gonna set the food over on the counter." He places the plate next to the bottle of Crown, scoops up the bottle, and returns to the table. The men sit and Austin fills his glass to the halfway point. "You're sure I can't interest you in some?"

Charlie holds up his hand. "I'm good."

"I'm drinking it neat. The ice cubes where a little old. I got a new batch freezing, if you change your mind."

"It's kind of what I wanted to talk about."

"Come on, man..." Austin falls back in his chair. "More lecturing? I'm fine."

"You're not fine. I'm worried about you and the booze. I came over here under the guise of bringing food to check on you, and not to my surprise, here you are. Drunk again."

"I'm fine," Austin protests.

"I've been with you every night for the last ten days now, and it's been the same every night, black-out drunk. You're not fine. You're not healthy. Look at you. You look terrible...like a skeleton of Agent Brown. I'll bet you've lost ten pounds in the last ten days. I haven't seen you eat anything, except pieces of toast when we'd eat breakfast."

"Pshhh. I'm fine!" Agent Brown waves a hand at Charlie.

"I'm not going to sit here and preach at you. I've said my piece, but you need to know I'm here to help."

"I appreciate your concern, Charlie. And your discretion. And everything you've done and are doing. You are a true friend." Austin lifts his glass toward Charlie and takes a swallow. "Oh, I'm sorry, Charlie. I didn't mean it the way that looked. I'm grateful. Really." Austin sets the glass down for the first time since Charlie's arrival.

Charlie seethes inside over the mocking gesture, but keeps calm. "No sense in beating a dead horse. I'm not in a position to judge. I just have my concerns is all."

Austin places his hands flatly together as if in prayer, and dips his head as a martial arts fighter might do to show respect. "Again, thank you, Charlie."

Charlie looks around the kitchen and connected dining area, noticing for the first time, even after all of the dinners he has eaten here with Veronica, the harsh light of the overhead fluorescent bulbs. The kitchen is cozy, a bit on the small side, but with the original, white painted cabinets, its retro feel is comfortable. That idea is challenged in Charlie's head now. He thinks now maybe it's all in the company you keep that makes the environment. His company tonight is less than desirable.

The drink has found its way back into Austin's hand and he sips loudly enough to bring Charlie's attention back to the table. "I said I have something to discuss and it is true," Charlie finally whispers and pauses.

Austin's brow furrows, he tenses, and the highball glass clumsily clunks down on the table. "What is it? Elliot?"

"No...I...I was wondering about your story from the other night."

Austin relaxes, his lips parting with half a grin. "Oh, yeah. My tragic tale of despair and woe." His hand sweeps dramatically across and up as a dramatic actor would emote. The Canadian whiskey taking hold. "Orphaned as an eleven year old." Austin chuckles at his own ridiculousness. "What do you want to know?"

"You said you shot and killed your father...how...how did you...how did you get *rehabilitated*?

"Ah, rehabilitated! Great word," Austin nods in affirmation. "More over, you want to know how a killer like me might end up as an FBI agent and so-called 'productive citizen.' That is an excellent question." Austin pours two fingers of whiskey into his highball glass. "Definitely worth exploring."

"It just seems...weird and all," Charlie voices softly, trying not to offend.

"I hear some skepticism in your tone there, Charlie. It's ok, I have a hard time believing it myself sometimes." Agent Brown leans back. He crosses his legs out in front of him, relaxing. "Those juvenile records were, and are sealed. Juvenile. Pshhh. I was eleven years old. I was a child. Nonetheless, those records might as well not exist. I don't have a criminal record."

"Were you charged?" Charlie's eyebrows rise in curiosity.

"Not so much charged. Let's just say the legal system worked things out. I was 'institutionalized' for a year. Detained for some time. Stuck me in all kinds of psychological therapy. Crazy, huh?" Austin snickers at his pun. He drinks from his glass, ending with a smack of his lips.

"That's some story. But, don't you have to go through all kinds of background and mental testing and such to join the FBI?"

"Yes, but let me back up and fill in some blanks for you. All that stuff, water under the bridge. I was packed up and sent to live with my grandparents. My mom's mom and dad. You could understand my paternal grandparents not really wanting to have anything to do with me...you know, killing their son and all." Austin dramatically leans to one side. "When I say 'went to live with my grandparents' I really mean shipped off to military school."

The whole story bemuses Austin. He laughs routinely, appropriately punctuating his sentences, much to Charlie's bewilderment over such tragic circumstances. "Are you sure you don't want some?" Austin leans the bottle of Crown Royal in Charlie's direction. "It's really good."

"No, I'm fine," Charlie insists with a wave of his hand.

"What do I know? I've been drinking the cheapest vodka. Maybe it's not actually so great, everything is relative. Anyhoo, where was I? Oh, yeah. My grandparents were old. They didn't want to raise a kid. They didn't have the energy for a twelve year heading into his teenage years." Austin laughs and shakes his head. "I don't blame them."

"You want some water or something?" Austin points to the sink and stands. Before Charlie can respond, Austin is up retrieving a glass and filling it with water. He returns to the table and places the glass in front of Charlie.

"Thanks." Charlie takes a sip.

"Technically, I'm not drinking alone now." Austin tips his glass toward Charlie and sips. "But, what could have been better for me than military school in my situation? Western Reserve Academy? Ever hear of it? No?" Austin shrugs. "Grandma and Grandpa paid about half, I got a scholarship for underprivileged children, again given my circumstance, how would I not get a scholarship? It's a pretty high-falutin school. Put me on a pretty good path."

Charlie listens to the inebriated man in front of him talk, seemingly emboldened by the alcohol. It boggles his mind to hear someone in such an authoritative position to talk so candidly about pain and suffering.

"It couldn't have worked out better for me. After graduation, four years enlisted in the Air Force. That *actually* finished the job of raising me. I was mature by then."

Austin sips slowly at his glass. "Mmm, this is good stuff. That cheap vodka was starting to wear me down in those stuffy motel rooms. I can't thank you enough for this," Austin flips his hands in the air and looks toward the ceiling a moment. "This feels like home. Make sure you thank Veronica again."

Austin gets up. "Let me get you some more water."

Before Charlie can react, Austin has his glass and is filling it at the sink. "It's already nine o'clock. You know what? I'm going to warm up that plate."

Austin returns the glass of water to Charlie and grabs the plate. He shoves the plate into the microwave sans foil. "What'd you say, three minutes on fifty percent?"

"Yup." Charlie sips his water.

Austin punches buttons on the microwave and it beeps accordingly. He returns to the table as the microwave hums in the background and he resumes his story seamlessly. "I had two years of college credits upon exiting the Air Force. Couple years at Ohio State studying criminal justice, virtually the simplest degree ever, with a minor in computer science, all paid for by the GI Bill and I was set. Before I even graduated the FBI came knocking. One of my computer professors had a friend at Quantico and she recommended me, unbeknownst to me mind you. When two suits in dark sunglasses showed up at my apartment to talk to me, I thought somebody was punking me."

The microwave chimes and Austin retrieves his food. He sits. "I can't believe I never told you all this before."

Austin digs into his food. His head bobs in satisfaction. "Oh, my goodness. This is delicious! I haven't' had something like this in months."

"Well," Charlie pushes himself up from the table. "I'll let you eat then."

Austin washes down a mouthful of food with his whiskey. "Thanks so much, Charlie. You guys are the best."

Charlie watches uncomfortably as the man sitting in front of him drinks whiskey as if it is water. "One other thing. Saturday, I'd like to have you come with us duck hunting."

Austin freezes mid-mouthful. "Huh?"

"I don't know about you, but I'm mentally exhausted and there's nothing like getting outdoors to clear your head. Remember the flocks of ducks I pointed out to you on the way back?"

"Mmm-hmm," Austin affirms as he chews.

"Well, there's nothing better than huntin' ducks 'cept maybe eatin' them corn fed mallards. Makes my mouth water right now."

"I don't know, man." Austin swallows skeptically. "I've never hunted anything. I don't' have equipment."

"That's not an excuse. Between me, Claude, and Nat we could outfit a small army."

A twinkle flickers in Austin's eye. "You know what? This sounds great. I'll do it!"

"There's only one thing that I ask."

"What's that?" Austin cocks his head suspiciously, pausing mid-lift of his drink to his lips.

Charlie flips a thumb at the glass in Austin's hand. "You're going to have to go easy on that stuff. We got to be up early, and I want you functional."

Austin sets his glass down without a drink. "Ok. Yeah. I'll handle it."

"I can't have you impaired on Saturday morning, shotgun in hand." Charlie's head shakes slowly.

"Don't worry." Austin waves away Charlie's cautionary words.

"I'm at work the next couple days, but you call me if something comes up."

Austin points a finger at Charlie. "And vice versa." Austin is still mindful of his drink on the table. He glances from Charlie to the glass and back to Charlie. He stands and moves to Charlie, hand extended. "Thanks again, Charlie."

Charlie reaches out his hand. Austin grabs his hand and pulls him into a hug, catching Charlie completely off guard. An off-balance Charlie hears Austin whisper in his ear, "I owe you."

Chapter 18
The Boy

Sleeping in a strange bed is not an issue for Austin. He is oblivious to the new, temporary quarters of Veronica's house. A half bottle of Crown Royal and sheer exhaustion will have that effect. Austin breathes deeply, asleep in the back bedroom. The uneventful night comes to a screeching halt with a thump from the kitchen that is just loud enough to register with Austin. He remains still, only his eyes open and adjust to the darkness. He sees a sliver of light permeating the bottom of the bedroom door. It only takes a moment for his deeply ingrained FBI training to kick in, even under the influence of alcohol.

"Somebody's here," Austin whispers to himself. In his mind, it can only be one person. "Elliot," he hisses the name aloud.

His eyes note the time on the clock, 2:00 o'clock in the morning, as he reaches for his pistol between the clock and the lamp on the nightstand. He rolls from his bed staying low. Moving to the bedroom door, he glances down the hallway. A shadow moves across the faintest of light emanating from the kitchen. Austin eases from the bedroom, his back flat against the wall, he inches down the hallway, gun held head-high next to his cheek. His heart pounds and he wipes at a bead of sweat on his forehead with the back of his hand.

Austin's mind is flooded with thoughts, racing to a conclusion that this is closure, a final showdown. Veronica had said it just a few hours ago, she was bait. The Deer Slayer had been lured in. The element of surprise is on his side, the Deer Slayer is expecting a woman, not a trained law enforcement officer. A careless bump in the darkness by the intruder has shifted the element of surprise Austin's way even further. At a snail's pace he proceeds, back to the wall, down the hallway. Agent Brown holds his weapon with a death grip. He is hyper aware of the pistol in his hand and he re-grips the gun, the checkered handle feels good in his palm. His mind goes over every step, a preview of what to do. Confirm target. Center mass, nothing fancy. Fire until target is down. The mental checklist is short and his mind reviews it again. He is going to end this case here and now.

The light in the kitchen is from the open refrigerator door. The dim appliance bulb reveals a Native American boy, no older than thirteen years old, rummaging through the fridge. Austin relaxes, shoulders slumping as he lowers his weapon. A wave of relief mixed with emotion and confusion washes over him. He flicks on the kitchen light, "What are you doing, Boy!" Austin growls.

The young man nearly falls to the floor in fright, slipping on the linoleum as he backs away in a scramble. His hands shoot up in the air and a soda can falls from his grip. The fridge door slams shut as he backs into the kitchen table, staring up at the man dressed only in boxer shorts holding a gun at his waist. "Don't shoot," the boy cries out nearly in tears.

Austin points the pistol at the boy. "Do you know how close to death you were?" he punctuates each word with the gun in his hand. His speech is slightly slurred, tinged with alcohol. "I almost shot you."

The gaunt boy with shoulder length, dirty hair is trembling. He is bent back over the table trying to keep his distance from the gunman. "Please...I was just trying to find some food. I knew Ms. Lewis moved out. She used to give me some food. I'm hungry." Tears flow from the boy's eyes. "Please don't...don't shoot me," he pleads. "I'm just hungry..." His voice trails off, lips quivering. "I just needed something to eat," his voice is weak, barely a whisper.

"Take what you want," Austin orders, lowering the gun. He waves the pistol at the fridge. The weapon comes up again trained on the boy. "You almost gave me a heart attack!" Austin drops the gun to his side. He looks at the ceiling, a moment of thanks to God for not shooting the boy.

"I'm sorry," the boy apologizes, his voice cracking. "The front door was unlocked, and like I said, I just came to get some food. I knew Ms. Lewis moved out and was hoping she left some food."

"You can't just walk into peoples' houses," Austin yells for emphasis, pointing the gun at the boy. "You'll get yourself killed!" Austin lowers the weapon. "Take some food and go. There's some deli meat in there. A whole bag. There are buns on the counter. Take 'em."

The boy grabs the bag of sliced turkey and closes the fridge door. He fumbles with the bag of buns. "Just take 'em all."

"I'm so sorry," the boy pleads.

"Just go." Austin waves the gun toward the door.

Austin follows the boy to the front door. The ashamed boy walks with his head down and steps outside giving only a glance back. Austin notices the boy's clothes are dirty and notes again how emaciated the boy looks. "I'm sorry," the boy mumbles.

He bolts off the porch, leaving on a dead sprint across the lawn, away from the street light and into the darkness. Agent Brown breathes deeply. He notices he's holding his breath again as the boy runs away. His hands tremble, the adrenaline fading quickly. "What the hell?" He questions aloud. He holds his chest; there is a pain, a stabbing pain, just under his sternum. He begins to weep, a shuddering sob at first. Feelings overwhelm him. Feelings he has not had since Jeannie died. His own self pity has overpowered any level of sympathy or emotion for anyone else. Seeing the pathetic plight of the boy breaks down a mental barrier. He cries, tears flowing freely over his cheeks, wiped away by the cold steel of the Ruger in his hand. Only then he realizes he is still holding the gun as he stands in the doorway. Staring into the darkness in which the boy had disappeared, he closes the door. Austin vows to do better, shutting the door literally, and symbolically, on the past two months.

Chapter 19
Back To Work

Bureau of Indian Affairs Police Headquarters – Sisseton, South Dakota

The BIA Police Headquarters is situated on the west side of Sisseton on the south side of South Dakota Highway 10. There is a reason a passerby might think that the police station resembles a concrete bunker, because it is...sort of. In the tumultuous 1970's, the American Indian Movement, AIM, left its mark on the reservations. The U.S. Government, in its response to the chaos in Indian Country, routinely constructed bunker-like buildings as it replaced its post offices and police stations in the years following AIM. The theory was that these concrete building could serve as outposts and headquarters for government forces if need be. There was never a time these buildings served that peripheral purpose. They just stand as ugly monuments of a fearful, reactionary government. Take notice if you ever travel the reservations. Police stations with their razor wire-topped chain link fences surrounding the motor pool provide a sense of militarization, but the post offices look innocent enough.

For Charlie, it's a short four minute commute from his house to work. Depending on weather and traffic, it might push his drive to work up to six minutes. It's a far cry from big city life. Charlie parks his BIA Police Tahoe in the back of the building and enters through the secure door via a keypad and code. Charlie's foot steps echo off the concrete floor and walls of the empty hallway around the corner and to the front of the building. In the reception area, behind the glass, he passes Kathy Chasing Hawk at her post as administrative assistant. It's a kick-start for his day, interacting with the ever-ebullient twenty-nine year old, young lady. Kathy is short and plump. Her hair is that of a teased-out nest of a 1980's rocker, starkly contrasting with her no-nonsense pant-suited attire. "Good morning, Kathy," Charlie calls out. "Is Skip in?"

Kathy's voice is tinny, coming through the intercom system. "Hi, Charlie! Welcome back! It's good to see you! The boss is in!"

Charlie gives a wave to Kathy as he continues onto Skip's office. He knocks on the door and enters. BIA Police Captain Skyler "Skip" Kipp sits at his desk. Across from him is BIA Police Officer Jeremy Two Crow. The two men turn their attention to the door as Charlie enters, "Well, I'll be," Skip smirks. "The prodigal son returns."

Skip and Jeremy stand and shake hands with Charlie, welcoming him back. Both men are significantly shorter than Charlie. Skip is all Native American in appearance, reflecting his status as an enrolled member of the Sisseton-Wahpeton Sioux Tribe. His face is rounded and he has slightly buck teeth, giving him a look of a chipmunk. His hair is long, traditional, in braids today, and falling from each side of his head to his shoulders. His long hair is an exception to the uniform standard for Native American BIA policeman. At fifty years old his hair is still jet black. "Does your uniform still fit?" Skip questions with a laugh. "It's been awhile."

Jeremy Two Crow laughs along with his boss. He is the newest member of the BIA Police force in Sisseton. With less than two years on the job, he's young, looking like he could pass for a freshman in high school even at twenty five years of age. The former state champion wrestler in the 105 pound weight class is small, but extremely tough. Deceptively tough, as criminals underestimating the policeman's strength have come to find out on the Sisseton-Wahpeton Reservation. Word got out fast about the "Kid Cop" and nobody challenges Jeremy anymore.

Jeremy is an enrolled member of the Pine Ridge Sioux Tribe, but in contrast to Skip's traditional braids, he sports a crew cut.

Charlie grunts a laugh as he smoothes the sleeves of his shirt. Jeremy and Skip return to their chairs and Skip sweeps a hand toward an empty chair, offering Charlie a seat. Charlie waves away the offer. "No luck?" Skip questions.

Charlie's head tilts to the left. "Nope."

"Nothing at all?" Skip follows up.

"Signs point to cancer. He might be dying, hence this last hurrah. We tracked him to the Mayo Clinic. Your old stompin' grounds."

"I'm very familiar." Skip frowns.

"How is Helen?" Charlie asks.

Skip nods confidently. "Still in remission. We're still cautiously optimistic, knock on wood." Skip raps his knuckles on his desk.

"Sorta came to a dead end." Charlie scratches his head. "All the medical privacy stuff. Austin's gonna try an end run and call in some FBI favors. We'll get 'im sooner or later."

"Let's hope for sooner." Skip frowns. "If he's trying to go out with a bang, I don't want to be cleaning up a mess."

The conversation stalls and silence settles for a moment. "Well, what'd I miss?' Charlie holds up his hands in question.

"Nothing." Jeremy glances at Skip. "Pretty quiet."

Skip holds up a finger. "One thing I wanted to share with you guys. These domestic violence calls, don't go without backup. That's from the Regional Commander, not just me. They've had too many situations escalate. You call for backup."

Skip enforces his point holding eye contact first with Jeremy then with Charlie. The warning hangs over the quiet room until Skip's desk phone chirps. "Hi, Skip," Kathy's voice crackles through the speakerphone. "Deidre Sampson from Social Services is here to see Charlie."

"He'll be right there." Skip looks to Charlie with a smile. "Back to work."

"Excuse me, gentlemen." Charlie moves to the door. "I'll talk to you guys later."

Chapter 20
Social Services

The police station's windowless conference room with its concrete walls is about as unappealing and uninviting as government architecture can get. The harsh fluorescent overhead lights bathe the room with a sterilizing glare. In an attempt to lift the décor, an orange, red and yellow sunburst at one end of the room painted on the cream colored wall is a feeble attempt at best. Each of the warm colors of the sunburst is represented by a stripe about four inches wide encircling the room. The sunburst and its stripes are a product of Kathy's creativity and donated supplies in order to make the staff meetings a little less unbearable.

Charlie sits across the conference room table from a stout, curly-haired woman wearing large, round, heavy-framed glasses. She is Deidre "Dee" Sampson, social worker. The plain looking woman is professionally dressed in her pinstriped pant suit. Middle age is setting in on Deidre, her face sagging a little, but she wears no make up and looks fine, natural. Charlie has known Dee since his first year on the job. He has worked with this consummate professional many times in dealing with family strife on the reservation. He knows he can count on her. "Thanks for meeting with me, Dee," Charlie begins the conversation. "How are things?"

"Good. It's nice to come to Sisseton under a little more relaxed conditions than usual."

"Speak for yourself."

"Touché," Dee laughs.

"Do you want me to call Courtney and see if she can join us?" Charlie reaches for his cell phone.

"I don't think that'll be necessary. I've had a conversation with the judge, and she's amenable to continuing the status quo with Haley. Has there been any word on her father..." Dee looks down at her notes, "Mr. Rodney Hopkins?"

"No there's no news," Charlie mumbles before clearing his throat. "Haley's been through the ringer with her stepmom and sister murdered. Throw that on top of her career-criminal father, the poor kid needs all the help she can get. Her father's off the grid."

Dee adds more notes to her pad. "There was only one question I couldn't answer. And the judge...she seemed stuck on it: What is Mr. Charlie LeBeau's interest in the case?" Dee puts down her pen, clasps her hands, places her elbows on the table, and leans her chin on her hands as she looks across the table at Charlie. Charlie shifts uncomfortably. He leans back in his chair, slouching a bit. Dee smiles. "I have to say, I'm curious myself."

Charlie stands and closes the partially opened door to the conference room. He returns to his seat and scoots close to the table placing his elbows on the table, mirroring Dee across from him. "I care about Courtney. We had a relationship a few years ago." Charlie pauses and gathers himself. "Is this conversation confidential?"

"Absolutely."

Charlie clears his throat. "Good, I'll tell you then. It was just revealed to me that Courtney's daughter is actually my child. It's a complicated situation. Courtney was in college in the Twin Cities, and our long distance relationship didn't last." Charlie lowers his head as he thinks how to continue. "Let's just say she and her husband had no idea that I was the father until there was a medical situation with Brittney, Courtney's daughter. Blood types didn't match...well, you get the picture. Now I have a vested interest in Courtney and her daughter...and any foster child like Haley in my daughter's life."

"Oh, I see." Dee picks up her pen and makes a note on the pad in front of her.

"Nobody knows any of this." Charlie waves his hands back and forth. "Except me, Courtney, her ex-husband, and Courtney's mom. But, her mom has Alzheimer's, so she knows, but her Alzheimer's' confuses her. That's how I found out. Courtney's mom blurted it out when I was dealing with Haley's situation and I visited them out in Big Coulee." Charlie runs his hands through his hair, agonizing as the stress builds with the details of the story. He stares down at the table. "Veronica, my wife, also knows. I just told her. Courtney hasn't even told Brittney yet. I don't think."

"Oh, dear, Charlie. You're dealing with a lot."

"We're trying to figure out how to deal with it all, like telling family and friends. It's awkward right now, keeping all these secrets."

Dee reaches across the table and pats Charlie's hand in a comforting gesture. "I'm sorry to hear all this, but I think I have some good news for you. The judge has asked all the parties to come in for a closed hearing. She wants to hear from you, but it should merely be a formality."

Charlie looks up, puzzled. "That's it?"

"Yup. The interim title will be removed from Courtney's foster parent status, and she'll have full custody of Haley...unless the father returns."

"I see no chance of that happening."

"She should be all set then."

Charlie smiles for the first time, "Thank you."

"You're very welcome, Charlie. I'll be in touch for the family court date." Dee reaches across the table and grabs Charlie's hand. "It'll all work out. I know you, Charlie."

Chapter 21
The Lead

Skip is at his desk flipping through pages in a folder when Charlie enters the captain's office and closes the door behind him. "What was that about?" Skip immediately questions barely looking up from the folder.

"You know, Dee from Social Services. We're still trying to straighten out Haley and her foster parent status with Courtney."

"Oh, yeah. How's it look?"

"Good."

Charlie flops down in the chair across from Skip's desk. "How 'bout you?" Skip continues to flip through loose pages in the folder in front of him. "Everything ok? Veronica? Married life?"

"So far, so good. I really need to thank you and Jeremy for keeping an eye on things while I was gone."

"Don't even mention it." Skip pauses his review of the folder a moment and glances at Charlie before resuming the page turning. "What I really wonder about is your honeymoon. You get married and then go spend ten days in hotels with Agent Brown. Who married who?" Skip laughs and steals a glance at Charlie.

Charlie rolls his eyes. "What? You been talkin' to my dad? I got the same line of questioning from him."

"I'm just messing with you."

"I know." Charlie stands. "I better go take care of some business. Ten days off. Plenty of emails to look at and calls to return."

"Don't worry about anything. We got your back," Skip roundly declares.

Charlie moves to the door and stops. "Yeah, I might need to bolt if we get any leads."

"Don't worry about it."

"Thanks, Boss." Charlie opens the door, but hesitates. "Did I tell you about the motorcycle?"

"What motorcycle?"

Charlie flinches. His eyes go to the ancient poster of John Belushi from Animal House on the wall. He smiles at the latest iteration mocked up by Kathy. John Belushi in his classic black and white poster wearing the sweatshirt that simply says "COLLEGE" is now adorned with construction paper. The colored construction paper forms what appears to be a school crossing guard uniform and in Belushi's hand is a construction paper sign. Distracted by the poster, Charlie pauses a moment, "I like the new Belushi."

Skip laughs and tilts his head a moment at the poster. "What about this motorcycle?"

"Shoot!" Charlie exclaims. That's the one solid lead we ended up with and I forgot mention it."

What about it?"

"According to the prostitute we talked to..."

"Whoa, whoa, whoa. Timeout." Skip holds his hands in a t-shape. "Prostitute?"

"Yeah, we had tracked Elliot via the face recognition software at the airport and he rented a car under the name of Eli Benton. We ended up finding that car at a motel. We sat on it for a few days hoping Elliot would show, but he was gone. When we talked to the hooker, he gave her the car to use for the rest of the month. He purchased a motorcycle and was gone." Charlie holds up a finger. "A fancy motorcycle. A Ducati. We need to be on the lookout for it."

"I'll let everyone know." Skip purses his lips. "We'll get 'im."

Chapter 22
The Gift

Night haunts Austin. Alone as a guest in Veronica's house it's a repeat of every night previous since his wife's death. Tonight he sits at the kitchen table, plastic pint bottle of vodka in hand. The overhead kitchen light fills the room with its cool illumination. He stares ahead at the refrigerator, his mind numbed by alcohol, but still unable to forget. Of all the memories that won't drown under the vodka, it's the words of the doctor, "There was nothing we could do."

The phrase rings hollow in Austin's ears. The television in the living room is nearly muted, but the late night talk show images and sounds provide a background distraction, and Austin glances at the screen. Taylor Swift is performing her song "Style" on the television. He twists the cap from the plastic bottle and guzzles the last ounce and a half from the container, eyes fixed on the TV. Replacing the cap, he chucks the bottle at the kitchen trash can. It bounces harmlessly onto the linoleum. "Nothing they could do," Austin whispers aloud as he stands on wobbly legs. Staggering to the fridge, he extracts a green bottle of beer. Twisting the cap without success, he realizes he needs a bottle opener. His eyes catch the time on the stove clock, 11:45.

He focuses on a drawer, opens it, and closes it. Opening another drawer he is frozen. He sets the Heineken bottle on the counter and reaches into the drawer. He carefully picks up a miniature Stanley utility knife attached to a key chain, extracting it from a jumble of pens, paper clips, and an assortment of other household tools. He stumbles back to the table, weak in his knees. Tears fill his eyes.

Even in his cloudy mind, the memories of fifteen years ago flood back as if it were yesterday. The memory transports Austin in time:

In a crowded McDonald's restaurant during the rush of lunch hour, Austin sits across from his beautiful wife, Jeannie, "Happy first anniversary, Honey." Austin smiles, reaches into the pocket of his sports jacket, and slides a small, neatly wrapped gift topped with a bow across the table. Austin grabs the burger wrappers and napkins out of the way.
Jeannie tries to frown, but can't, "We agreed. No gifts."

"I know. Don't worry. It's nothing fancy."

Jeannie opens the gift, revealing a miniature Stanley utility knife on a key chain. "You remembered?" Jeannie's' face beams. "Thank you! It's perfect for my crafts."

She leans across the table and kisses her husband.

The memory is over and Austin sits at the kitchen table. The knife and its key chain stretched out before him. He sits in his chair, elbows on his knees, hands holding his chin. The knife is just a few inches from his face as stares at the black and yellow lettering on the handle. Tears fall freely on the table.

Like a coiled spring, Austin is up from the table. He moves to the living room and retrieves his pistol from its holster resting on the coffee table. His eyes catch a glimpse of a man in a suit on the talk show, hands flailing in the air. Back to the kitchen table he sits, placing the pistol next to the key chain, bumping the knife and kinking the chain. His fingers work to straighten the tiny links and once complete, he scoops up the gun in a fluid motion and sticks the barrel in his mouth. His sobs are muffled by the semi-auto Ruger .40 caliber. "Jeannie," Austin's whispering word is garbled.

He cocks the pistol and holds the weapon in his mouth for a half minute, but his finger never moves to the trigger. He can taste the metallic gun barrel and the oil on his tongue. His thoughts catch up to his actions, and he removes the gun from his mouth, easing the hammer down, he stares at the gun. He fumbles the pistol onto the table with a crash, mumbling to himself, "This is Veronica's house. I can't..."

Austin stands up quickly, sending the wooden kitchen chair backwards with a thud. He staggers to the living room couch and falls face-first into a pillow where his wailing cries are muffled.

Chapter 23
A Second Opinion

Mayo Clinic – Rochester, Minnesota

In the glowing sunshine of the clinic's waiting room, Elliot Kauffman relaxes on the comfortable couch. His arms extended either side of him across the back of the sofa, his head tilts back so his face can feel the full warmth of the sun through the skylight above. The waiting room is more like an arboretum than a medical facility. The waiting area fills with a variety of people as the first appointments of the afternoon arrive. Above the patients, speakers emit the hypnotic instrumental intonations of The Bob Crewe Generation's "Music to Watch Girls By." Just before 1:30 pm a nurse reads a name from the stack of papers held on her clipboard, "Mr. Benton."

Elliot Kauffman, a.k.a. Eli Benton doesn't move at first. His eyes are closed and he is enjoying the sun. "Mr. Benton," the nurse calls again. Elliot's eyes flutter open as the name rings in his ears. He raises his hand as he stands and smiles at the young nurse. He follows the young woman to the exam room, exchanging small talk. Elliot is rail thin, sporting a shaved head in contrast to his bushy beard.

Inside the exam room, Elliot sits on the exam table. He is shirtless and his torso bares the scars of recent surgery. Elliot breathes as instructed by a Middle Eastern doctor, a young man in Elliot's mind, Doctor Ahmed-Mustafa. Elliot thinks back to his scheduling of the appointment when he had heard the name and questioned the receptionist on the doctor's background. Pakistani, if Elliot remembered correctly. No matter, Elliot just wanted to know what the prognosis was. The first opinion had been a death sentence, now was the moment of truth, was there any chance for survival?

The doctor listens carefully with his stethoscope before finally removing it from his ears and stowing the instrument in the pocket of his spotless, white lab coat. "You can put your shirt back on," the doctor instructs without a hint of an accent.

Elliot dons his light, flannel shirt and buttons it. "Your lungs sound the way they should be expected to sound given your condition. I do not have positive news for you, Mr. Benton. Have you been prescribed oxygen?"

Elliot nods. "I advise you to use it." The doctor retrieves a computer tablet and begins tapping and scrolling through menus on the screen. "Let me show you the MRI results." The doctor expands the digital images on the screen. "It's not good."

Elliot holds up a hand. "Lay it on me. I've already been told once. This is just a second opinion."

"I'm sorry. I would agree with the initial diagnosis."

"Four months or less?" Elliot questions. "That's what I was told."

The doctor's mouth twists in thought. "A time frame given is merely speculative, but, yes, based on my experience, four months give or take."

The doctor touches areas on the tablet screen and they glow in red. "Here, here, and here. These are masses, larger than images taken from just a month ago." The doctor tilts his head. "Were you a smoker, Mr. Benton?"

"Nope, just unlucky I guess." Elliot frowns. "I blame it on the oil wells they set on fire over in the Gulf when I was there."

"You were in Desert Storm?" The doctor focuses on Elliot's face.

"Yup."

Elliot's memory flashes to images of himself with his helicopter crew. He fires his .50 caliber machine gun at the crowd of Iraqi soldiers below as the chopper climbs, straining for altitude. The soldiers below shoot back with small arms fire from pistols. Soldiers crumple to Elliot's bullets and the helicopter bucks as the pilot guides the aircraft way. The roar of the engine, the rotors and the gunfire are muffled by Elliot's headphones. "God damn it," the pilot curses. "What are we even doing out here?"

Elliot looks down and can see bullet holes in the floor of the chopper to his right.

"I'm sorry, Mr. Benton. We will do the best we can. Are you in pain?" The doctor's words halt the battle memory and Elliot's eyes meet the doctor's. "I am recommending we halt all chemo and other treatment. Pain management and comfort is what we are dealing with at this stage."

Elliot reacts with a disinterested shrug. He has other plans in mind.

"You are going to have to make some end of life decisions. Would you like to have your wife..."

Elliot interrupts, "I'm not married. I am alone."

The doctor stops what he's doing on his tablet and looks at his patient. "Do you have arrangements? Hospice?"

"I have plans," Elliot replies flatly.

"Is there anything else I can do? Do you have any questions?" The doctor presses the button on his tablet and the screen fades. He sets the computer aside.

Elliot pushes himself off the exam table. "I'm good. Thank you for your opinion. I feel a weight has been lifted."

Elliot extends his hand and the doctor shakes it. Holding Elliot's hand the doctor's eyes water. "I'm sorry. My brother..." the doctor chokes on his words. "My older brother was a surgeon with the Army in Desert Storm. He too, died of lung cancer, similar to your case. Much too young. You have my deepest sympathies."

Elliot grips the young doctor's hand as he looks at the man in a different light. "Thank you, doctor."

"I'm so sorry," the doctor repeats again. "Best of luck on your journey."

Elliot manages a smile at the use of the word "journey." Now there's a word he hadn't heard or considered to this point as he has processed and contemplated his death. "Journey." Yes, that's the word he liked and would rely upon.

Chapter 24
Pillow Talk

Charlie's House – Sisseton, South Dakota

Charlie lies next to Veronica in bed. His eyes are closed, arm over his face to shield the light from Veronica's night stand as she reads. "Did you see the weather on the ten o'clock news tonight?" Charlie questions.

"Cloudy and windy." Veronica lowers her book, marking her page with her finger as she closes it. "Perfect for going out in the morning. Claude told me that you guys would have a whole pile of ducks to clean tomorrow."

"I admire his confidence," Charlie's tone has a touch of sarcasm. "We'll definitely get some, but I'm not sure what constitutes a 'pile' of ducks."

"I'm looking forward to trying some."

"Your wait is almost over." Charlie speaks with his eyes closed, arm still resting over his brow. Agent Brown is supposed to go with us."

"You asked him?"

"Yeah, and he reluctantly agreed. He's never hunted before, so he balked. Didn't have a gun. Didn't have clothes. I assured him that we have plenty to get him outfitted." Charlie pauses. "I have my doubts that he'll be here, and if he is, I question whether he'll be sober that early in the morning." Veronica listens without interrupting. "His drinking is out of control, man. I don't know how much longer he can continue."

"Did you say something to him?" Veronica questions.

"Sure. I gave him the spiel about alcohol and the reservation. He didn't want to hear it. He's like, 'mind your own business.'"

"Do you blame him? What he's been through?"

"Yeah." Charlie's eyes open and he rolls to his side, facing Veronica. "I'm going to talk to him again and again. Whatever it takes. This hunt tomorrow, maybe help get his mind off things."

Charlie reaches out and places his hand on Veronica's belly. "And you? How are you feeling, Mommy?"

"I'm fine. Never better. I'm still in a little disbelief I guess." She places her hand atop Charlie's. "How was work? First time back in a while, must've been a long day."

"No, it was good to see everybody." Charlie snuggles closer to Veronica's side. He closes his eyes, "Dee from social services came by regarding Courtney and Haley. Sounds like there's going to be a formal hearing in front of a judge."

"You have to go?"

"Yeah, the judge wants to hear about my relationship with Courtney, since I'm the star character witness, being with the police and all."

"Ooh," Veronica winces.

"No, it should be alright. It's a closed hearing. Confidential in family court."

"So, your relationship with Courtney your..." Veronica pats Charlie's hand. "Correction...our new daughter, Brittney, can come out on our own terms."

Charlie smiles. "In theory. I don't think Courtney has even told Brittney yet. But, once word gets out, watch out, gossip'll be like wildfire."

"Might be some rough conversations for people in the near future."

"Yup. More to come on that story. I look forward to reading about it in your newspaper."

Veronica playfully slaps at Charlie's hand. "Stop."

"How's Kelli doing? You hand over the reins yet?"

"She's perfect."

"Nat's going to come help you too," Charlie's voice is fading.

"I don't know about that," Veronica's tone is doubtful. "He's got basketball starting up."

Charlie provides his counter-argument. "That's the beauty of his early commitment, no pressure on the season. He can relax and lead a semi-normal teenager life. I'm so glad he already signed. When he gets to college, basketball will be a full-time job for him."

"That's true," Veronica agrees. "It's not stopping him from working out. Every free moment, it still seems like he's out in the driveway shooting baskets."

"We also have a secret weapon available to help you, if needed," Charlie states, voice rising.

"What's that?" Veronica scoffs.

"You mean, who's that. My dad, of course! He can help you."

"I'm not that desperate yet," Veronica laughs. She leans down and kisses Charlie.

"Good night," Charlie groans. "We're going after those ducks pretty early tomorrow."

"You want me to get up and make you guys breakfast?"

"No. You take it easy."

Charlie rolls over and grabs his cell phone from the night stand. "I'm going to text a reminder to Austin. I have my doubts he'll be ready."

Charlie types a message and sends it. Before he can set his phone down, it lights up with a reply. Charlie reads the message aloud, "He says he'll see me 'bright-eyed and bushy-tailed.' I'll believe it when I see it."

Charlie leans over and kisses Veronica. "Good night."

"Night." Veronica opens her book and gets back to her reading.

Chapter 25
The Hunt

Charlie, Nat, and Claude are in the driveway loading gear under the sparse illumination of the yard light. A vehicle's lights cut through the darkness and Charlie pauses a moment to observe the headlights shine down his driveway. He mumbles quietly to himself, "By God, he made it."

Austin pulls his Chevy Malibu into the driveway, parking behind Charlie's old Ford Truck. He kills the lights and exits the vehicle. "You look no worse for the wear," Charlie remarks. "You ready?"

"I told you I'd be here bright-eyed and bushy-tailed, and I'm here. You got some clothes for me? And a gun?"

"Gun's in the truck already. Come over to the shed and we'll get you some camo. How are your boots?"

Austin kicks at his black, military-issue boots. "Eh, these are good enough. If it was colder, I might need something different."

Charlie points a finger at the truck, "I got some boots in the truck. We might suit you up in the chest waders. You can be our retriever."

"I have no problem with that. Glad to do what I can."

Austin tries on a jacket and it is adequate. In a few moments they are loaded up.

"You guys can go; Austin and I will follow you." Charlie waves Nat and Claude toward his truck. He turns to Austin. "Sorry, buddy, not enough room in my truck for the four of us. You'll have to drive your car."

"I keep telling you, Uncle Charlie," Nat says with a tone of disappointment in his voice, "you need to upgrade to one of those extended cab trucks."

"Someday..." Charlie replies, his voice trailing off.

The convoy drives in the darkness. Austin and Charlie travel without conversation. The radio plays Gordon Lightfoot's "Sundown" followed by "Solsbury Hill" by Peter Gabriel. When the funk song "Early in the Morning" covered by Robert Palmer comes on the radio, Austin finally comments, "Well, this song is right on the nose."

Low clouds block out any hint of starlight. The wind gusts, buffeting the vehicles as they head west on Highway 10, toward Lake City. Turning north on Highway 25 it is just a couple miles to an approach where they leave Austin's vehicle. Austin and Charlie climb in the back of the truck and hunker down the best they can out of the wind. They hang on as Nat bounces down the two-rut trail. Austin can see the cattail-lined lake for the first time as they parallel the shore. The first hint of the sunrise to the east provides the faintest of light and Austin notices the sea of tall grass surrounding the trail they jostle down. The grass bends and straightens, rustling in the wind, appearing like swells in an ocean. He looks around seeing two distant farmyard lights miles away. They seem to be in the middle of nowhere. Nat brakes hard and Austin jerks forward with a grunt. "We're here," Charlie calls out with the glee of a child.

The eastern sky is steadily giving way to a lighter gray on the horizon. The rolling hills provide uneven silhouettes as Austin takes in the surroundings, trying to landmark his position. "Come on, let's get those decoys set out." Charlie looks to Austin. "Get those waders on. I'll toss out the decoys and you can wade out and fine tune their positions."

"Sure." Austin unlaces his boots and sits on the tailgate wriggling into the waders.

He can hear splashes barely audible in the wind. The north wind pushes steadily. It is overcast and breezy, potentially a perfect day for a duck hunt. The splashes come more quickly as Nat assists Charlie in tossing the plastic mallard duck decoys into the water. The flexible, curved, lead weight straightened from their position around each decoy's head find the lake bottom and nylon cords unwind and jerk the plastic birds into place.

It is quiet, conversation is minimal. Charlie and Nat throw out the last decoys and Austin wades in the water, and under the direction of Charlie, positions the decoys in an inviting pattern. Nat is assisting Claude with the blind. The two men carve out an opening in the cattails. They break off the dried, brittle plants and stomp down an area where they can hide. The whistle of wings overhead draws everyone's attention. There is enough light now to see the silhouettes of ducks passing above.

The decoys set, Charlie calls out, "Everybody got their guns? Ok?" Charlie waits for affirmation and upon receiving notice, he provides the next order of business. "Nat, go hide the truck. I'll get everyone situated in the blind."

The shore of Middle Lake transitions from a boulder strewn shallows to a rocky beach, and finally to sandy shoreline. The sand gives way to twenty to thirty foot swath of cattails around the shore. Charlie inspects the blind in the hollowed-out cattail opening, "No, too far. We need to be in the sand." He points, "Let's get that dead tree hauled over. We've got our old surplus camo net we can drape over it."

Charlie and Claude work on the camo netting. "Austin, move the decoys over so we got a landing area right in front of the blind, half to the left, half to the right."

"Will do," Austin calls out as he splashes into the water.

"What do you think, Dad?" Charlie questions.

"Should be good. Ducks will be coming off the main lake, back into the cove and cattails a little more out of the wind. They'll be coming right by us, see the dekes, and drop in."

Charlie pauses his fastening the netting into the branches as another flock of thirty ducks whistles over. A scattered quack or two of the passing birds is mostly muffled by the wind. "This is the best time of day."

"You betcha," Claude agrees.

"I think you're right. Ducks should be streaming past, just like that," Charlie nods skyward as his fingers work the netting into the twigs to keep it from flapping.

More ducks pass over, and Charlie pulls a five gallon bucket into the blind and sets it down as seat. The blind provides camo from the lakeside, while they are exposed from the shore side. He sits on the bucket and holds his shotgun at the ready. He stands and shoulders the gun, testing his mobility within the blind. He swings the barrel from left to right and back again, practicing what a shot at a passing duck might be like. He sits down and leans his shotgun against the branches of the blind. "Yup. Perfect. No cover on the backside, but ducks won't be coming from that direction." Charlie raises his voice, "That's good enough, Austin! It's getting light enough to shoot. Come on!"

Chapter 26
Shooting Time

"Five more minutes," Charlie informs the group as he looks to the east. Nat joins the crew, returning from hiding the pick up near the remnants of the trees surrounding an old homestead. "Three minutes, Nat."

Nat acknowledges the time with a nod. He picks up his shotgun and chambers a shell in the barrel with a pump of the forearm on his 12 gauge Remington 870. He slides another shell into the magazine. "I'm ready."

The men move into the blind and watch flock after flock whip past the decoys. "Everybody ready?" Nat questions.

"Man, they weren't kidding about the ducks being thick out here." Charlie works the action on his semi-automatic Browning A-5 shotgun, chambering a shell in the 12 gauge. "You know how to work that shotgun, Austin?"

"Yeah, I got it figured out." Austin pumps a shell into the chamber of his Remington 870. "Nat showed me."

Ducks land in the decoys, but stay only a few moments, frightened by the voices and the men standing up in the blind. Claude breaks open his side-by-side double barrel shotgun, an old Winchester. He sticks a red 12 gauge shotgun shell in each barrel, closes the breach, checks the safety, and holds the gun at the ready. "What's the plan?"

"Ducks come in, we shoot them," Charlie replies smugly.

"I know that, hotshot," Claude remarks, annoyed. "But, what about after the sun rises and the ducks stop moving?"

"We'll worry about that later," Charlie flicks a shoulder in Nat's direction. "That's why we got Nat. If it slows down, we'll send him on walkabout."

Claude gives a thumbs up in the ever-increasing light. He hefts his gun. "It's close enough. Next flock comes by, I'm going to bust 'em."

Three medium-sized ducks swoop in, land, and leap skyward with a splash, scared by the men standing in the blind. The men observe the ducks a moment. "Hey, Dad." Charlie picks up his gun, "Why don't you let our guest here have the honors. He's never hunted before."

Austin protests, "Nah, let me watch and get the hang of it first."

Claude waves the comment away. "No such thing. We're going to sit back and watch you pop your cherry on your first duck."

"Hey," Nat points to the water. "Here comes some! Right on the deck. Get your gun, Austin!"

The men hunker down behind the blind as five bigger bodied ducks swing into the decoys, wings cupped, feet outstretched just twenty five yards out. Austin grips his gun. "Take 'em," Charlie orders.

Austin stands, picks out the biggest duck as the surprised birds flap their wings trying to backpedal and gain altitude. The receding darkness is split by the flames from his barrel, and the duck splashes into the water. Austin pumps the gun, picks out another bird and fires again at another duck climbing high in escape. The duck crumples, dead instantly. It tumbles down, smacking the water and temporarily swamping a decoy it lands next to.

"Holy cow!" Claude calls out. "We got ourselves a dead-eye Dick."

Charlie rests his gun against the branches of the blind and applauds. "You're a natural." Charlie points to the water. "You got the waders, get on out there and retrieve 'em. Good shootin'."

Nat claps a hand on Austin's back as he sets his gun down and exits the blind. "Impressive."

Austin is all smiles as he wades out, weaving through the decoys and their weighted lines. He hustles to get the furthest bird first as the wind pushes the bird toward the middle of the lake. He circles back and picks up the second bird. He returns to the blind and hands over a bird to Charlie. Both birds are drake mallards. "Two nice greenheads. Eighteen more and we're done. That one you're holding is perfect."

"It's beautiful," Austin says softly. He strokes the feathers with a gloved hand, fingering the curly tail feather. "It's amazing. Look at these colors. The green head. Iridescent. Look at the purply-blue bars on the wings. This is so cool."

"Wait until we get some light, those iridescent purple feathers will really pop. It's called the speculum. You should see them in the sun." Charlie holds up the other duck.

"What is that one?" Austin questions.

"The same, just an immature bird," Charlie remarks. He runs his hands over the mottled colored feathers.

Austin is mesmerized by the drake mallard in his hands. He inspects the bright orange feet, pulling on the legs and expanding the webbing to its fullest. He smiles a broad smile. Charlie can't help but grin himself. He gently sets the duck down on the sand, under the cover of the blind. Charlie slaps Austin on the back in congratulations. "Come on, buddy. Hand it over and get in the blind. Here comes another flock."

The sun rises and the crew nearly fills their limit of mallards with a few other types of ducks for good measure after an hour of steady shooting. The bag includes a perfect drake wood duck specimen brought down by Nat. "Uncle Charlie, get my picture with me and this wood duck." Nat excitedly hands his phone to Charlie. "I'm gonna post it on facebook."

"Are you sure you want to do that?" Charlie reluctantly takes the phone. "You know how vocal some of these anti-hunters are."

"It's a free country," Nat quips.

"Just because you can do it, doesn't mean you should do it," Claude pipes up.

"Yeah, listen to your grandfather," Austin joins the conversation.

"Just take the picture!" Nat insists.

Charlie takes a couple of photos as Nat flashes a proud smile while holding his prized wood duck. He hands the phone back to Nat who is immediately tapping away, adding a description to his photo uploaded to Facebook.

"Excuse me gents. I gotta take a leak," Claude announces.

In a few moments Claude returns with a bundle of cattails. "Whatcha got there, Claude?" Austin questions.

"I'm glad you asked," Claude begins. "I wanted to demonstrate the techniques of our peoples' duck hunting two hundred years ago."

"What are you talking about?" Austin asks, puzzled by the non-sequitor. "What's with the cattails?"

"These here cattails were the prime tool for harvesting waterfowl, by the ancient bands of my people." Claude drops the stack of long stems and leaves. Grasping three leaves he begins to braid them together as everyone watches. "What they did was weave together these cattails, scientific name *typha*, into strands of thin ropes." Claude finishes braiding the four-foot long piece together and hands it to Austin. "They'd do this until they would have enough to assemble into nets." Claude braids together another section of twine-like material. "My understanding is that in the fall the ducks were even more plentiful than they are now. They didn't have the fancy firearms to hunt with, although gunpowder has been around a long, long time thanks to the Chinese. Instead the young braves would set traps in the small sloughs or coves of the big lakes. They'd get their nets in place and lay in wait. They had some pretty intricate contraptions for catching large numbers of waterfowl at a time. They needed some of their braided bison ropes for strength to pull the nets closed on their larger catches."

"That's interesting." Austin inspects the braided fibers. "Not very durable though."

"That's the beauty of it. They were disposable nets. One season and whoosh, threw 'em away. My people were nomads; they didn't have room to pack these bulky nets as they moved from hunting grounds to hunting grounds."

"Amazing." Austin is awestruck.

"Who taught you all that?" Charlie asks.

"This was all shared with me by Titus Korman, you know him. He's up in Veblen."

Charlie laughs. "Yeah, that guy's so old, he probably used this method to hunt ducks when he was a kid."

"Wasn't that long ago," Claude continues. "Used to be a lot more ducks, before the farmers drained all the sloughs. It's hard to believe there were even more ducks than there is now. The people made use of the ducks' eggs in the spring. People associate the bison with Indians, but I'm of the mind that waterfowl had just as an important role."

Charlie points across the water. "Hey, get in the blind, here comes some more."

Chapter 27
Montevideo

Montevideo, Minnesota

In the parking lot of the Viking Motel on East Highway 7 in Montevideo Minnesota, Elliot stiffly dismounts from his motorcycle with a groaning effort. The Nordic culture touches everything in the area. From the Minnesota Vikings football franchise to the lutefisk capital of the world, the Scandinavian roots are pervasive, and frankly, Elliot has grown weary of it. He shakes his head at the motel sign with its cartoonish depiction of a bearded man with horned helmet and blonde braids either side of his head.

Elliot rolls his neck trying to shake the stiffness from the long ride. The motel front desk is managed by a young, disinterested woman, and she hands Elliot a key to his room, turning her attention back to her romance novel before he can say "Thank you."

Elliot steps toward the door and knows he is at risk of bothering the clerk, but asks, "Any suggestions on something to eat?"

She doesn't' look up from her book. She extends her arm and finger, pointing across the parking lot. "Pizza Ranch is good."

"Thank you," Elliot mumbles. He smiles to himself while going out the door. There is something about this young lady with her round face and short haircut that triggers a memory.

Back in the parking lot, Elliot grits his teeth and pushes his motorcycle rather than starting it. It's less than a hundred feet to the parking space in front of his room and he figures the effort might help loosen his stiff muscles. With a few grunts he accomplishes the task and he unstraps his life's possessions from the back of his bike.

In his motel room he finally sheds his helmet and rain gear. The weather is a perfect metaphor for his mood and his life. The 200 mile ride from Rochester to Montevideo was completed in a steady drizzle. There is nothing like riding a motorcycle in wet, drizzly conditions. If that doesn't put your body on high alert and give you that white-knuckle driving experience, nothing will.

Elliot is exhausted. He can see the Pizza Ranch sign out his window and he pulls the curtains closed. A hot shower brings some relief to his aching body and his attention turns to supper.

*　　*　　*

Elliott trudges the fifty yards from his motel room to the restaurant. The Pizza Ranch is a Midwestern, family-friendly restaurant franchise found in medium-sized communities in the Dakotas, Minnesota, and throughout a few other Midwestern states. Montevideo is a relatively small town of about 6,000 people in west-central Minnesota. Located in Chippewa County, it is the county seat, and one of many communities primarily focused in the agricultural services business. Farm fields surround the town and it is bisected by two river valleys, the Chippewa River and the Minnesota River. It is a bucolic Midwestern town, but today it's a little gloomy with the cold front pushing rain through the area.

The Pizza Ranch, as its name might indicate, is a place that serves pizza, but there's a buffet with chicken, salad, and other fixings. Elliot finds the food satisfactory and the sparse crowd is a perfect setting for him to stay anonymous. He finds a booth next to a window and sits down with his salad from the buffet line. The background music of the restaurant catches Elliot's ear. It's a strange version of a Beatles' tune, a Smooth Jazz cover of "Dear Prudence" by Jeff Lorber. Elliot smiles to himself as he is able to recall the song from the recesses of his brain. The eclectic mix of music overhead bounces to the 1980's mainstream pop and "Do You Believe in Love?" by Huey Lewis and the News. The music is a temporary distraction and his mind returns to its preoccupation while the wind is blustering outside. Large drops of rain pelt the window next to him. He can see the traffic passing on Highway 7. Elliot picks at his food as his mind wanders through what's next.

Chapter 28
Not Nostalgia

Elliot lies in bed, hands behind his head, staring at the ceiling. The thin curtains don't block the street lights and his brain interprets the random illuminated textures on the ceiling into images: a man fishing, a dog's head, a bat with wings outstretched. His thoughts settle on his mortality. He's a dead man. The digital clock radio alarm suddenly activates, filling the room with the high volume plaintiff warbling of "Baby I'm a Want You" by Bread. "Jesus Christ!" Elliot shouts as he fumbles to turn the alarm off.

It takes a few moments for Elliot's heart to settle to a normal beat as he stares at the ceiling. His mind drifts back to his previous thoughts. The cancer has got him in its grip. What's left for him? The question bounces through his head. Nothing. He's satisfied with his time on earth, it wasn't wasted. He thinks of the motel clerk, and his lips part with a smile. She reminds him of his first kill. It is not necessarily nostalgic. It is an analysis of his technique and effort that shaped everything and everyone else he killed. Yet, it turns out, there is unfinished business.

Elliot closes his eyes and remembers:

Veblen, South Dakota – 1980

In the lunch room of Veblen High School, an eighteen year old Elliot Kauffman sits at a table with his group of friends. Lunch room is a stretch of the term. It is the gymnasium with tables pulled out of the wall to accommodate the one-hundred-or-so students. Voices echo in the gymnasium, bouncing off the tile floor and concrete block walls. It is loud in the gym with, the constant din of conversation. Directly across from Elliot is Shanice Williams. She is eighteen years old also and shares Elliot's class schedule. Shanice is a little on the heavy side, but her pretty, dimpled, round face goes along way to make her an attractive option in the limited pool of high school girls. Elliot holds her hand across the table, drawing a few annoyed glances from his fellow diners. Shanice is Indian. She is very light skinned with minimal features to give away her heritage. Her mother is an enrolled member of the Cheyenne River Sioux Tribe and so is she.

"Hey, Shanice," Debbie Thompson calls out from across the table. "You wanna go into Sisseton tonight and catch a movie?" Debbie is Shanice's best friend. She is Native American on her father's side. Both are members of the Crow Creek Sioux Tribe. She is attractive, dressed in her skin-tight blue jeans and denim jacket. Elliot had set his sights on her, but she was cool to any of his advances, so Elliot settled for Shanice. Shanice is a willing partner in any of his desires.

Shanice giggles at Debbie's suggestion. She eyes Elliot and blushes at her thoughts. "Elliot and I have plans for tonight. Maybe next weekend."

Elliot squeezes Shanice's hand in affirmation. Debbie half stands and reaches across the table toward Shanice's ear beneath her Dorothy Hammel haircut. "Love the earrings, girl."

"Duh, of course you do. You gave them to me."

The bell rings and the students move out. "Four more hours," Elliot groans as he pushes himself up from the table.

"I can't wait," Shanice grins and winks.

*   *   *

"Where are we?" Shanice questions. She guzzles the rest of her wine cooler. Classical orchestral music, Beethoven or Bach, plays on the FM radio.

"Kirschner's. It's the old gravel pit for their ranch. It's just a few miles south of town."

"We won't be bothered, no?"

Elliot hands Shanice another wine cooler. "It's the middle of nowhere. No."

Elliot and Shanice are parked facing east in the isolated coulee along the Prairie Des Coteau. No lights are visible except a couple farmyard lights in the distance and the half moon overhead. Elliot's 1970 Ford truck is warm and he pulls Shanice close and drapes an arm over her shoulder. The blanket seat covers are cozy. Elliot grabs the wine cooler from Shanice. He loosens the cap and hands the bottle back to her. She drinks as she watches Elliot lean forward and open the glove box. He fishes out plastic baggie and her eyes widen. "You got some?" Her excitement uncontained.

"You don't know hard it was to get these. My buddy in Sisseton knows a guy in Fargo. These mushrooms have traveled a long ways."

"Can I have some? Please?" Shanice is begging. Her voice whines, as that of a four year old child.

"You finish your drink. I'll get started." Elliot grins. He opens the baggie and digs out a hefty chunk of mushroom. He palms it and pretends to put it in his mouth and chew. He makes a face and grunts, "Blah, tastes awful."

Shanice tips the bottle to her lips and gulps half the wine cooler, racing to ingest it. Distracted by her haste to finish the drink, she doesn't see Elliot replace the mushroom in the bag. Shanice takes a breath and returns the bottle to her lips, downing the rest. "I think it takes a few minutes for the mushrooms to take effect," Elliot mumbles and leans back in his seat, relaxing.

"Well, give me one! I finished my drink."

Elliot opens the bag and digs out a piece. Shanice reaches for the mushroom, but Elliot brushes her hand away. "Open up."

Shanice giggles and opens her mouth. Elliot places the spongy lump on her tongue and she chews. "Ooh, they don't taste good. Like dirt or something."

Shanice closes her eyes and leans back. "What are we listening to?"

Elliot snuggles closer to Shanice, brushing her ample breasts with the back of his hand. "I'm sorry. It's public radio. It's the only thing I can tune in. We're kinda blocked by the Coteau."

Shanice breathes a deep sigh. "Don't be sorry. I kinda like it. It feels good with my wine cooler buzz."

Elliot leans forward and kisses her on the mouth, his hand slipping under her shirt. "That feels good. I feel...good," Shanice speaks into Elliot's mouth as he kisses her.

Her eyelids are heavy. They are closed and the power of the hallucinogenic mushroom begins to take effect. A feeling of euphoria descends upon her.

"Can we get your pants off?" Elliot asks.

Shanice's fingers go to the button on her tight jeans. It's a struggle to get her fingers to work and Elliot assists. The chore continues as she peels down her pants. The operation stalls at her zip-up boots. "Oops. I forgot about my boots," her voice is breathy and distant.

Shanice is out of sorts now, but she clings to Elliot kissing him and interfering with his efforts to strip her clothes off. Her face is painted with a smile, her words are slurred. Elliot works to get her boots off and onto the floor, she is pushed up against the passenger- side door. Her jeans are removed and Elliot traces the mound of pubic hair just below her silk panties. He inspects her creamy thighs and legs, tinted an eerie greenish hue by the dashboard lights. "You ready?" Elliot asks.

"Mmm-hmm." Her answer is more of a groan than speech.

Elliot plunges his hand into her underwear. His finger finds the moist opening and he works rhythmically, brushing her clitoris. "Oooh," Shanice moans. She pulls at her panties and they tear. "Take them off," she orders.

Elliot works the tattered delicates down her legs. He whispers, "I want you from behind." He works his finger deeper into the warm, velvety receptacle.

"Whatever you want, baby," Shanice breathes the words.

"I can't do it in the truck. We'll have to go outside. I'll put the tailgate down and bend you over it."

"Ok." Shanice's head lolls as Elliot works his fingers insider her and she is in complete euphoria.

Elliot breaks contact with Shanice via a kiss. "Come on, I'll go around to your side and get you."

Elliot moves around the truck, lowers the tailgate, hustles to the passenger side, and opens the door. "Oh, oh my God. These mushrooms are wonderful," Shanice calls out as the door opens.

Elliot works to get the virtually limp girl out of the truck. "It's a little chilly."

Elliot's comment is an understatement. It is a cool fall evening. Not cold, but not suited for nakedness. "Can you help a little?" He asks. "Let me just carry you."

It's a struggle to get her to the back of the truck. Elliot has her over his shoulder. Shanice giggles. "I can help."

She reaches for Elliot's zipper and brushes her hand against his bulging erection. Elliot flinches, nearly dropping the girl. "No, not yet. Let's get you on the truck."

It's a bit of an exertion, but he accomplishes his mission. Shanice is on his jacket spread over the tailgate. She spreads her legs and Elliot works his finger back between her thighs and finds her button. She stiffens with a moan. Elliot looks around warily. He hadn't planned for

Shanice to be this vocal. She sounds like an animal. "Shhhh," Elliot pleads. His eyes dart from side to side, looking into the darkness.

He works another finger over her vulva. She moans more loudly than ever, and he looks around, cautiously, full of paranoia. His hands are covered in fluid, a drip trickles down her leg. He works with one hand to loosen his belt and unbutton his jeans. "Shhhh," he urges again.

"Oh, God!" Shanice cries out as Elliot pushes her button with his finger.

"Sh. Sh. Sh," Elliot urges.

Elliot manages to get his blue jeans and boxers to his ankles. He pulls his hand from Shanice's crotch and rubs his erection with the cream on his hand. He can feel her juices on her thighs as he pushes her legs apart. He strokes himself, hardening his member. "Ok."

He manipulates her into position and inserts his penis into her welcoming vagina. Her body becomes rigid and relaxes. Elliot pumps, faster and faster. "Oh. Oh. Oh. Oh! Oh!" Shanice cries out louder and louder in rhythm. Her voice gives way to guttural groans. Elliot scans the area side to side. It is a distraction and he can't climax worrying about the noise. Shanice sticks her ass out further and further, wanting more. Elliot grits his teeth and pours it on, faster and harder.

Elliot's eyes close. "I'm going to come."

"Go ahead. Go. Go!" Shanice shouts the command.

With a moan, Elliot withdraws his cock and ejaculate shoots across her exposed buttocks and shirt. "Whoa," Elliot gasps, wiping a bead of sweat from his forehead.

Shanice pants like a dog, unable to speak as her body shudders in cold and excitement. Elliot hurries to pull up his boxers. He tucks his still firm and dripping penis into his shorts and pulls up his pants. "That...was...amazing," Shanice is finally able to speak, the words trembling out of her mouth.

Elliot looks around in the dark. Starlight and the partial moon provide a mysterious mood. "You were great."

Elliot pulls Shanice, limp as a ragdoll, into his arms. "I can't stand up," she mumbles. "You fucked me so hard and so good."

Elliot kisses her lips. Shanice's eyes are still closed, heavy from the mystical powers of the mushroom. She receives the kiss and tries to speak, "Oh, Elliot, can we do that again?"

Elliot stumbles to hold up the girl. Shanice wraps her legs around his waist and kisses him. His hands move to her neck and he presses on her throat, choking her. The hyoid bone in her neck snaps immediately under his thumbs. "Sure," Elliot snarls through gritted teeth as he squeezes harder.

Shanice puts up little resistance, incapacitated by the mushrooms. Survivor instincts finally kick in and her eyes pop wide open in crazed bewilderment. She grips Elliot's wrists, her fingernails dig into his skin. Elliot loses his balance. They fall to the ground, Elliot landing on top of the woman, squeezing the life out of Shanice.

"Aurrrrgh!" The pain of the fingernails digging into his wrists causes Elliot to press harder and Shanice's grip subsides.

Her muscles relax and her arms fall harmlessly to her side. Minutes pass and Elliot still holds his grasp tightly around her neck. Sweat pours from his forehead and he wipes at his drops of sweat fruitlessly with his shoulders as it runs down his nose. He wants to be sure. The plan has been near perfect. Her body convulses and goes completely limp. It's all over and Elliot stands over the body of Shanice, his breath coming in gasps from the exertion and adrenaline. "Sorry," he mumbles.

His breathing is slow to recover, as if he has just run a fast paced mile. He is soaked in sweat, shaking and shuddering, now beset with chills. The cool air exaggerates his shuddering and his teeth chatter from the cool temperature and his excitement. He reaches down and grabs for Shanice's lifeless arm, takes hold, and drags her about fifty yards to a three foot deep pit freshly dug into the gravelly soils. Her grave.

"Damn it," he curses aloud. The grave doesn't seem deep enough as he pushes the body into it.

He shakes his head and looks around, surveying his surroundings. The paranoia is an amazing rush. Has anyone witnessed this murder? No. There's nobody around for miles. Maybe somebody heard her screams while having sex? No. Can't be. The questions bounce through Elliot's head as he scans the darkness. He steps into the hole and bends over the body. He pulls the left earring and then the right earring from Shanice's ears. His first trophy. He stares down at the earrings in his hands. There is just enough light to see the objects. They go into the pocket of his jeans.

He returns to the truck, casually now. He retrieves the rest of Shanice's clothes and boots. He snaps his finger as he remembers to grab her small purse. He returns to the grave and tosses the boots and clothing into the hole. The purse follows, but not before he digs twenty-two dollars from her wallet. It's back to the truck again, this time for a shovel. He returns to the grave looks down for a moment, leaning on the shovel. His wrists hurt and he sees the blood on his hands and handle of the shovel. "God damned fingernails."

He feels the first twinge of pain from the gouges on his wrist. He curses again as he tosses the first shovel-full of rocky soil over the body.

Chapter 29
Alibi

Elliot lies in the bed of his hotel room. He rubs the scars on his right wrist, his personalized souvenir from his first kill. The fingernail scratches became festering wounds, a typical by-product of dirty nails. His wrists healed, but the four symmetrical scars on each arm became permanent reminders of that night, where he can take himself any time with a simple brush of his fingertips on the bumps. It happens now and his heart quickens. Thirty-plus years later, his heart still reacts to the memory. It had been too easy.

Elliot remembers again:

Sisseton, South Dakota – 1980

Elliot's plan had functioned like clockwork to this point. Shanice was in the ground and he was in Sisseton. Standing outside the SISTON Movie Theatre, Elliot waits for the crowd to emerge from Clint Eastwood's "Any Which Way You Can." Elliot had made a point to see the movie on his own the week before at a matinee. He would be able to talk all the plot points for the sequel to the surprise hit, "Every Which Way But Loose."

The movie is over and patrons file out of the cinema with their groups. Debbie Thompson and a group of her friends shuffle out the doors of the theatre. Elliot falls in behind Debbie, "Hi, Debbie." He calls out meekly.

"Elliot?" Debbie turns around. "Where's Shanice? Were you guys at the movie?"

"I came by myself," Elliot whines. "Shanice stood me up. She called and said something came up. Do you know what's going on?"

Debbie is puzzled. "I haven't talked to her since school."

Elliot holds his right wrist with his left hand, both wrists ache from the wounds. Bandages cover the gashes, and athletic wrist bands cover the bandages, all the rage of fashion. "I don't want to hold you and your friends up. Just let me know if you talk to her." Elliot turns away, but stops and faces Debbie again. "She's pissing me off. Do you think she finally did it? Ran off to California?" She's always threatening that she was gonna."

"I'm sure it's nothing." Debbie frowns, but quickly turns it to a smile. "Maybe she got her period and is just holed up at home." Her comments bring the slightest chuckle from Elliot. "Hey, why don't you come with us?" Debbie inquires. "We're going to get root beer floats at the A&W?"

Elliot shrugs, "I guess."

Montevideo, Minnesota – Present Day

Elliot lies in his bed in his motel room, eyes closed, a grin creases his face. He returns his hands behind his head, interlocking his fingers. He opens his eyes and stares up at the ceiling. He unclasps his hands again, needing to touch the scars one more time. His eyes strain to see the tiny bumps, scar tissue from Shanice's fingernails all these years later. He can't see them in the dark. Elliot unleashes a snicker as he whispers, "Barely a question from the police a month after Shanice disappeared, and Debbie even kissed me that night. I was good."

Elliot coughs painfully, chest in spasm. His breathing is labored and he groans as he shifts in bed, the smile gone from his face. "God damn it." Elliot coughs again, mucous gathering in the back of his throat.

Chapter 30
Squatter

Sisseton, South Dakota – BIA Police Headquarters

Charlie is at the duty roster, signing out on the dry-erase board. He's done for the night and replaces the cap on the marker as Skip approaches. "Hey, Skip, remember when this used to be a chalkboard? Back then it was a little dust that we had to put up with. Now, we got the fumes from the markers. Who knows what those chemicals do to a guy."

Skip laughs. "You want to go back to the old days?"

"Who doesn't? The job seemed like a cakewalk back then."

"You done for the day?" Skip questions.

"Yeah, but I'm on call though. First up."

Skip wags a finger at Charlie. "Remember, nobody goes to a domestic situation without a backup."

"Well, you make sure you tell the rest of the crew."

"How's Austin? I saw him at the Alco."

Charlie scoffs, "That surprises me. I thought that the only place you'd find him is at the liquor store."

"That bad, huh?"

"Pretty bad. He's coming over for some roast duck tonight. We took him up to Middle Lake up by Dumarce and shot a bunch of ducks. Got his mind off things for a moment. He seemed to enjoy it."

Skip nods. "Hey, I just got a call from my Uncle Titus."

Charlie chuckles, and throws his head back. "I think I had a phone message from him."

Skip clucks his tongue. "You know how he is, Charlie. He said he hasn't heard from you."

"I know. I forgot. I listened to his message, but I haven't called him back. Trying to catch up. He wasn't specific about what he needs. Did he tell you?"

"He said there's somebody squatting in a boarded-up house a couple blocks over from him. The old Raymond house. You know how he is about this kind of stuff."

"Titus, the Neighborhood Watch." Charlie rolls his eyes.

"That's the way he is. He is insisting that I not be involved since he is reporting it. He has a real thing about nepotism, me being his nephew and all. So you're up. He wants you to check it out."

"It's no problem, Skip. I'll take care of it."

"Thanks."

"I'm outta here. Roast duck awaits! I'll see you later."

Chapter 31
Roast Duck

Charlie's Mobile Home

The dining room table is set. Charlie, Veronica, and Claude hover around the kitchen waiting for the decision. Charlie looks again at kitchen clock on the stove, then to the wall clock. Austin is a half hour late, everyone is hungry, and the clock shows six-thirty. "That's it. Let's eat," Charlie grumbles in disgust.

Charlie puts on the oven mitts and pulls a large roaster from the oven. "You wanna give him one more call?" Veronica asks meekly.

"Too late. He won't pick up. He won't respond to a text. Face it, he doesn't want to be here."

Claude fills the glasses on the table from the water pitcher. "More for us," he chimes in quietly.

Charlie shoots a glare at his father and Claude shrinks down trying to avoid eye contact. Charlie takes the cover off the roasting pan and steam billows from the five ducks inside. "I'll take him some leftovers and check on him later."

Everyone inhales the wafting scent of wild duck. Nat is up off the couch sniffing the air. He turns off the TV and heads to the table. "Smells great."

"Let's eat," Charlie commands. "Be careful of any stray pieces of shot."

"I got the biscuits." Claude scoops up the plate of Pillsbury Grands. "Nat, grab the potatoes."

"Is that everything?" Veronica questions. "Everyone, just sit. We'll say grace."

It's a scuffling of chairs on the linoleum and everyone is seated.

Chapter 32
If Not For Them

Veronica's House

Charlie stands on the front porch holding a plastic bag full of leftover duck. He watches Austin through the window adjacent to the door. The frosted glass contains multiple diamond shapes of clear glass that Charlie can peer through. Agent Brown sits alone at the kitchen table in the dimly lit room. Charlie listens. There is no sound. No radio, no television. Austin Brown is alone with his glass of clear liquid. He swirls the half-filled tumbler round and round. Charlie spots a large bottle of vodka on the table, a third of it gone.

Charlie continues to watch Austin. The man in the white t-shirt and blue jeans leans his weight on the table, resting on one elbow, glass in hand, swirling about. His other hand continuously runs through his hair. Periodically, his head dips down, and he sips from the glass. Charlie interrupts the operation with a light knock on the door. He can see Austin flinch, hand going to the small of his back where he would normally have a weapon holstered. He's not armed and he looks to the living room a moment where his holster sits on the coffee table. His head swivels to the door and he pushes himself up form the table. "Who is it? Is that you, boy?"

"It's me, Charlie." Austin opens the door and escorts Charlie to the kitchen. "How come you didn't come over?" Charlie questions with a whine, sadness in his voice as he sets the plastic bag on the counter. "I brought you some duck. Potatoes. Biscuits. It's delicious, by the way."

Austin retrieves his glass from the kitchen table, snatching it, annoyed by Charlie's' tone and question. "You know. I just...can't." Austin puts the glass to his lips and finishes the rest of his drink.

Austin looks pathetically at the bottle of vodka on the table. Embarrassed, he picks up the bottle and splashes the liquid into the glass, filling it half full. "Why don't you sit down, before you fall down," Charlie orders. Austin flops into the chair, spilling a few drops of his drink on the table. He wipes his hand over the mess and licks his fingers, repeating the cleaning process. Charlie watches in pity. He pulls out the chair opposite

Austin and eases down, resting his elbows on the table and eyeing the drunken man across from him. "Can't you see I'm trying to help you?" Austin won't look at Charlie, first looking down at his drink, then focusing his attention on the front door, wishing to himself that he would be left alone. "How long is this going to go on?"

Austin doesn't answer, instead taking a drink from his glass, a gasping gulp. Charlie leans back in his chair, disgusted with the situation, he folds his arm in disapproval. The antics draw a response from Austin. "I'm sorry. I'm a terrible host." He pushes the bottle toward Charlie. "Would you like some? I'll get you a glass."

Charlie shakes his head at the man, eyes narrowing in anger. "I'll ask again, how much longer is this going to go on?" Austin drinks, looking again at the front door, eyes focused far away. "To tell you the truth," Charlie continues, "I don't see it lasting much longer. You're going to be dead." Charlie stares at the man across the table from him. Austin won't make eye contact, instead he sips from his glass. "What?" Charlie questions mockingly. "Does what I said make you angry? Because it's a fact?" Austin looks at the bottle of vodka, reaches for it, and splashes more into his glass, spilling again. "What about your daughters?"

The question hits a nerve with Austin, and he finally meets Charlie's eyes with his. "What about them? They are better off with their grandparents."

"That's not true," Charlie objects, his voice going higher in protest. "Those kids need a father."

"You don't know, Charlie. That was her thing. The kids." Charlie notes the glassiness of Austin's eyes as the man takes another swallow of vodka. "I'm not a good parent. Never was, never will be. I loved her..." Austin's voice cuts off abruptly. Charlie is confused. His eyes are locked with Austin's. "I love my kids, but they were hers. She did everything for them. I was just a breadwinner. I was gone all the time...with the job. They need a woman, their grandmother to..." Austin looks to the door remembering...staring beyond the door. The first tear flows from his eye, unabated, across his cheek to the floor. Austin doesn't even try to wipe at it. "I really didn't want kids, but I loved her so much...I did anything and everything I could to make her happy." Tears stream from his eyes and he does nothing to even acknowledge them. "That's all over now."

"Yes, taken from you by Elliot. I need you," Charlie is adamant. "If you won't quit drinking for your daughters, quit drinking for me. I need you to help me get Elliot and to protect my family." Austin flinches. The words are a punch to the gut. He looks at the glass in his hand and drinks.

"I need you sharp. At your best if Elliot comes...and he'll come." Charlie pleads, "I have a family, and I need your help."

Austin throws his head back and drinks. His head nods as he pours down the vodka. He lowers the empty glass. "You're right. I'll try." Austin sets the glass on the table and wipes his mouth. "I'll try."

Chapter 33
Dom

Austin is up early. He leans on the rail of the front porch. He drinks coffee and breathes the crisp morning air, his coffee steams in the chill. The water vapor hangs in the air, combining with the vapor from his coffee as he exhales. The still air is crisp and his lungs sting as he inhales deeply, trying to ease the damage from the night before. The yellow light of the early morning sunshine casts intricate shadows on the front lawn and street. This morning is the perfect environment for another bargaining session with himself. Austin swears a promise to himself that he will stop. Stop drinking himself to sleep every night. It's the same guarantee he's made to his body countless times over the last two months, and a failure in negotiations over and over. He promises himself that this time will be different. This is the day the deal will take effect.

His internal conversation screeches to a halt and his body stiffens. A young man, no a boy, is walking along the sidewalk, through the shadows of the trees. It's the boy he chased out of his house. He had been on Austin's mind ever since that night. He could have easily killed the boy in his drunken stupor. What had stopped him? Maybe it was his dulled reflexes that had saved him from a quick decision that night.

The boy stops on the sidewalk in front of the house and reaches in his pocket. Austin reacts, reaching for his pistol in the small of his back. He holds his hand on the gun, "Whaddya want?" Austin is uneasy; he re-grips the pistol in his hand behind his back.

"Take it easy." The boy holds up his hands in a calming fashion. "My name is Dominique Thompson...Dom." Austin inspects the boy suspiciously, every nerve on high alert. The boy has his long hair pulled back into a ponytail. He's wearing a gray hooded sweatshirt under a thin windbreaker. Blue jeans and Converse basketball shoes round out his wardrobe, not enough clothes for a cool morning. Dom slowly reaches into his pocket. "Man, calm down. I have some money. I want to pay for the food I took and to say I'm sorry for just walking into your house."

Austin's shoulders slump as he relaxes and lets out a breath. "Forget it. Keep your money."

Dom walks forward, extending the money in his hand. "I ain't no thief. I want you to know that."

Austin glances around the leaf-strewn yard. He had promised Veronica he'd take care of it and yet, here the boy in front of him stands calf-deep in leaves. Austin signals the boy closer with a flick of his wrist. He can see the prideful boy has to give him the money. If he is to have any dignity left, he has to give the man the money, a five dollar bill. "Why aren't you in school?" Austin asks as he takes the money from the kid.

The boy just shrugs. Austin sips his coffee and cocks his head, looking the boy up and down. "I'm not interested in school," Dom finally replies.

"I'll tell you what," Austin holds up the five dollars. "I got your money, and now I'm going to call the police and see about you getting back to school."

"Go ahead," Dom scoffs. "We'll see if they can find me." He starts to walk away, kicking at leaves in the yard.

"Hold up," Austin calls out, and the boy stops. "I'll make you a deal, a pretty good deal I think. I'll give you your money back and thirty bucks more..." He has Dom's full attention. "Plus, I won't call the police and report you as a truant."

The boy looks up at Austin on the porch with suspicion. "What do I gotta do?"

"See all those leaves you're standing in?" Dom looks at the yard and nods. "Well, all you have to do is go to school and when the day's over, come back here and I'll pay you to rake up all these leaves."

"Fifty bucks," Dom counters.

Austin laughs. "I don't think you're in a position to negotiate."

"Can't hurt to ask," Dom shrugs.

"I'll tell you what, forty bucks." Austin looks around the yard. "There seems like a lot of leaves. Plus, I'll cook us supper. Burgers."

Dom slowly walks back to the porch as he contemplates the offer. He stands in the yard below Austin, scratches his head, and extends his hand. "Deal."

Austin shakes the boy's hand, palming the five dollar bill and sticking it back in Dom's hand. "Hey," Dom protests, trying to push the money back to Austin.

"That's an advance. Use it for your lunch money. At school." Austin wags a finger at the kid. "By the way, my name is Austin Brown. It's nice to meet you, Dom."

Dom dips his head and holds up the five dollars, acknowledging Austin's gift. "Thanks, man."

Austin points a finger at the boy. "I'm going to call the school, and if you're not there, the deal is off. Get going, before I change my mind." Austin points at the school buses down the street. "Heck, you might not even be tardy."

Dom waves a hand at Austin, turns and jogs toward the school, kicking leaves up on each step through the yard until he reaches the sidewalk.

Chapter 34
All Points Bulletin

Sisseton, South Dakota – BIA Police Headquarters

Jeremy Two Crow sits at his cubicle checking email. Charlie sits across from him in the shared office space reviewing a file. For Charlie and all his fellow officers, the grueling part of the job is the paperwork. This includes filing the traffic tickets for the court. "We had another domestic at one in the morning last night," Jeremy comments quietly.

"Really? Who was it?" Charlie doesn't look up from his checklist.

"Our buddies over in Peever, the LeComptes."

"What is that? Three times this month?"

"Yeah. Worst part though was waiting for back up. It took Skip thirty minutes to get there to back me up. Things were pretty calm by the time we knocked on the door."

Charlie finally looks up from his paperwork. "We're going to have to coordinate better with the Sheriff's Department. If we have to wait for backup before even going to the door, somebody's going to be hurt or dead by the time we take action."

"I know what you're saying." Jeremy nods his head in agreement. "These domestics are a bitch to deal with. They turn on you in a blink of an eye. Suddenly the cop is the bad guy, and they forget what they were even fightin' about." Jeremy's eyes widen as he clicks on an email. "You gotta be shittin' me!"

Jeremy's exclamation catches Charlie off guard. "What's wrong?"

"I just saw the memo about the motorcycle and Elliot Kaufmann. What the hell?" Jeremy's voice is in a whine. "Why wasn't this thing a radio call out and all points bulletin?"

Charlie tenses, he tosses the file on his desk and gets to his feet, "I thought it was? You saw him?"

Jeremy flicks a hand toward his computer screen. "I was on patrol a couple nights ago and this motorcycle flew by at hundred-plus miles an hour. I never gave chase. There was no chance."

"Are you sure?" Charlie questions.

"Guy was wearing a helmet, but those motorcycles are pretty sick." Jeremy continues with a tone of disgust. "I recognized it as a Ducati right away."

"Where'd you see 'im?" Charlie asks.

"It was up by New Effington. Just routine patrol."

"Shit," Charlie enunciates precisely.

Chapter 35
High Alert

Charlie's House

Charlie stands in his driveway as the sun sets. He had spotted the ducks from the county road, even before he turned down the driveway to the house. A few hundred yards away, a couple thousand ducks circle the cornfields terraced amongst the trees at the base of the Coteau. The flock of ducks is a thick black mass, diving and darting in a single tornado-shaped cloud, then splitting into two funnel-shapes, twisting and turning, amorphous blobs in the sky. One flock touches down in the cornfield closest to the coulee momentarily, and then the rush of wing beats and the visual strobe effect of the flapping wings launch the birds back into flight. They circle and swirl about the cornfields, the sky turning red and everything in silhouette, as the waterfowl cruise the field looking for the perfect spot to eat.

Out of the corner of his eye, Charlie sees what looks like a coyote moving across the two-rut trail a hundred yards north of his house. The trail leads to ten acres of prairie grass the Hakken's mow and bale each summer. The bales provide a stack for Charlie's deer stand each fall. "What the heck?" Charlie questions aloud. "That's not a coyote. It's a dog," he whispers.

Charlie whistles and the dog turns and trots toward him. It appears to be a German Shepherd. The dog stops about 75 yards out, staring on at Charlie who whistles again. "Come 'ere, boy!" Charlie calls out.

The dog flinches and bolts into the tall grass and disappears into the shadows of the coulee. "Hmmph," Charlie grunts. He turns and heads to the house.

Inside the house Charlie finds Claude in the kitchen. "Hey, Dad, did you see all the ducks working Hakken's cornfield across the coulee?"

"Yeah. We'll have to hit that tomorrow night if they don't clean it out," Claude replies without looking up.

"Sounds like a plan. What are you working on for supper?"

"Pork chops. On the grill."

"Sounds good. "Veronica and Nat home?"

Hands full, Claude jerks his head toward Charlie's bedroom. "Laying down." He jerks his head toward the other end of the house. "Homework."

Charlie moves to Nat's closed door, knocks, and enters. "I need to talk to everyone in the kitchen a minute."

Charlie moves across the house to his bedroom, quietly opening the door. Veronica is asleep on the bed, but senses Charlie's presence and awakens. "Hi," she says while stretching. "What time is it?"

"It's supper time. Six o'clock."

"Good." Veronica finishes stretching and sits up.

"I need to speak to everyone in the kitchen for a minute. Can you come out?"

"Sure," Veronica responds with concern. "It sounds serious. What is it?"

"Just come out to the kitchen. I want to tell everyone."

"Ok. Just give me a second to freshen up." Veronica disappears into the bathroom.

In the kitchen Claude, Veronica, and Claude gather around Charlie. Everyone is silent as they note Charlie's solemn expression. They wait patiently, each meets Charlie's eyes as he glances at their faces. "I got some bad news at work today. Elliot was spotted on his motorcycle in the area a couple of days ago."

"The hell you say?" Claude barks.

"I'm sorry, I'm just finding out now. There was a breakdown in communications on our all points bulletin. Everybody needs to be on high alert. Nobody is out and about, or here at home, by themselves."

"Are you sure it was him?" Veronica questions.

"Jeremy reported it this morning. He freaked out when he saw the email." Charlie shifts his weight and leans on the kitchen counter. "He said the guy was wearing a helmet, but he knew the type of motorcycle. It's pretty rare around here and it struck a chord in him. I trust Jeremy's judgment. Again, we can't let our guard down. High alert."

Veronica wipes her eyes as tears form. "I gotcha." Charlie wraps an arm around her. "We'll be ok." Charlie wraps his other arm around Veronica and hugs her. "Changing the subject, anybody else see a black dog, looks like part German shepherd around the house?"

Claude perks up. "He's back?"

"I'll take that as a 'yes,'" Charlie mumbles.

"I saw him a couple days ago." Claude moves to the window and looks out, but it's nearly pitch dark. He pulls the blind shut. "I named him 'Zero.' I threw some scraps out on the driveway about twenty yards out and he would come running by, nervous as all get out, and try to snatch something on the run, stopping thirty or forty yards out." He reminded me of those World War II Japanese dive bombing planes, Zeroes."

"If they're Japanese planes you're thinking of, then it's more likely they'd be Kamikaze planes, the suicide pilots," Nat pipes up.

Claude waves a hand at Nat in annoyance. "I like Zero, his name is Zero."

"Well," Charlie intervenes in the argument, "we're not naming any dog yet. Why don't you try to catch him? Maybe somebody lost him. If you catch him, we can take him to Doc Miller and see if he's got a chip in him."

"If he doesn't, can we just keep him?" Claude smiles. "I'd like to have a dog. We could teach him to retrieve ducks and hunt up some pheasants."

"I'll think about it." Charlie pursues his lips. "First things, first. Everybody is on high alert." Charlie points a finger at Claude and Nat. "We'll worry about that dog later. Let's eat."

Chapter 36
Cornfields

"Glad you could make it," Charlie whispers.

"Me too. This is amazing," Austin replies in a husky whisper.

The men are hunkered down on the edge of a cornfield just a few hundred yards from Charlie's house. The sun is on its way down. The wind blows gently in their face as they look out over the meandering rows of corn terraced into the hillside of the Coteau. The irregular-shaped field is bordered by the coulees shrouded in leafless trees. The ducks have arrived, mallards, five hundred or more, in this flock that whiz by the men shielded by a clump of tumbleweeds they have pulled over themselves as they kneel in the tall grass that demarcates the field from the coulee. The rush of the wings squeak overhead, intermingled with feeding chuckles, the guttural quacks of the drakes, and the sporadic, raucous quacking of a hen mallard as the flock circles lower, looking for the perfect place to land and feed on the leftover kernels of corn.

"Unbelievable," Austin whispers again, keeping his head down to avoid the glare from his cheeks, eyes straining to see the birds.

"I know, right?" There is a smile built into Charlie's affirming question. It is a great feeling for Charlie to be able to share this experience with his friend and maybe, just maybe, break the downward spiral Austin suffers. "Next pass, we'll take 'em. On my call."

Another flock of 200 mallards joins the bigger group, dropping in from a half-mile high, the air rushing over their wings sounds like the roar of a jet in the distance. "Holy smokes," Austin whispers excitedly. "You hear that?"

"Yeah. Get ready."

The flock of about 800 birds swings over the hunters at twenty five yards, and the lead birds flap furiously, settling into the corn about thirty rows out. "Now!" Charlie orders and the men spring from their cover and fire three shots each. Birds tumble down to the left and right, five, then six, finally another duck glides down about one hundred and fifty yards away.

"Nice job!" Charlie high fives Austin, who grins like a child.

"I'll go get that far one!" Austin is bursting with adrenaline as he breaks into a trot. "Wooo!" he shouts as he pumps his fist heading toward the downed duck.

Charlie loads two shells into the magazine of his shotgun, works the bolt on his automatic and feeds another shell into the magazine as he walks picking up the downed mallards in the rows of corn. A loud booming shot from Austin's direction makes Charlie swivel to see what happened. A duck falls, and Austin jumps in celebration. A straggler has fallen to Austin's shotgun.

*　　*　　*

About two miles north of where Charlie and Austin are, Nat and Claude stand in the tall grass along a harvested cornfield. They turn to face the booming report of gunshots. "Charlie and Austin," Nat states as he scans the sky.

"Better get down, those ducks will be coming our way," Claude replies as he takes a knee.

Nat stands a moment longer, straining his eyes in the fading light, searching for ducks. He follows suit, kneeling beside his grandfather, leaning with both hands on the barrel of his shotgun, anxiously looking for ducks. The men disappear into the tall prairie grass along the cornfield. This field is more open than the hillside ground where Austin and Charlie hunt. The long straight rows extend north and south from Nat and Claude, from where they are positioned on the west side of the plot. The breeze from the north is not in perfect favor, but the freshly harvested corn will attract the waterfowl. A John Deere combine and tractor with grain cart rest at the far north end of the field along the paved county road. A semi-tractor with a grain trailer sits in the approach loaded with corn next to where Nat parked his pickup truck. Claude had noted on their walk out to the cornfield twenty minutes ago the price tag of the equipment in the field. "Probably looking at the neighborhood of a million dollars of equipment right here."

Nat laughed, "Yeah, the poor Hakken brothers, is there anything they don't have?"

"Hey, don't begrudge their success. They've worked hard for what they got," Claude lightly chastised Nat as they had trudged through the corn stalks.

"Yeah, I know," Nat frowns. "The only question I have is: how did they get the land in the first place? Wasn't this all the reservation?"

"Point taken, young man."

Twenty five minutes later, and four hundred yards from the equipment, Nat and Claude wait in the grass as the light fades quickly. Ducks pour in from every direction. The flock from Charlie's field has merged with another thousand birds from the east. The mallards circle the cornfield, dipping and diving, forming a tornado-like cloud as they search for a place to settle and feed. "You ready?" Nat asks.

"On your call," Claude responds, staring at the flock swirling in front of him.

Ducks are landing fifty yards out. The bird's wings frantically back pedal as they ease in between the cornstalks. The flapping of wings emits a steady whoosh as the ducks land. Feeding calls and chuckles come from every direction as the birds continue to settle. The bulk of the flock is on the ground and the last mallards alight just twenty five yards from Nat's and Claude's position in the grass. "Now," Nat calls out as he stands and Claude rises beside him.

The surprised birds spring into the air. Nat picks out a fat greenhead pulls the trigger in the roar of wings. Both shotguns speak. Ducks rain down on the field. Nat fires again. Claude holds his fire after one shot. The hunters are both stunned at the ducks on the ground before them. "Holy Cow!" Claude reacts.

"Get that one," Nat orders. "The one with broken wing. There's two over here still alive. I'll get 'em."

The huge flock disappears into the red sky, heading west, chased from the area. Nat and Claude gather the wounded birds and dispatch them. The pile of mallards grows to ten and the two admire their handiwork. "Should I just go get the truck?" Nat questions. "Then we don't have to lug these things back."

"C'mon, man," Claude winces. "We're men, we can do it."

Nat reaches in his pocket. "Hey, I got some twine!"

"There you go. Cinch 'em up." Claude slaps his grandson on the back. "Nice shootin' by the way."

Nat laughs. "You too, Grandpa. I don't think there was a way we coulda missed." Nat raises his gun, re-enacting the hunt. "They seemed like they were two feet from my barrel. I only shot twice."

"I only shot once," Claude snorts. "Good thing we didn't unload. We'd a been fifty ducks over the limit."

"Here, hold my gun." Nat hands Claude his shotgun. "I'll get these things strung up. It's getting dark fast."

"We're not going to get 'em cleaned tonight," Claude looks at the darkening sky. "Get them so we can just hang 'em up and pick 'em tomorrow in the daylight."

"Will do."

Loaded with four ducks over each shoulder, Nat trudges along through the cornfield. "You ok, Grandpa?"

Claude has the twine over each shoulder, three ducks on either end. "No problems here. Slow and steady."

The cornstalks crunch under foot as they move toward the truck. "You hear that?" Nat stops and listens.

"What?"

"Shhh. Listen. Stop walking. Is that a motorcycle?"

Their hike is interrupted and they listen to the whine of a motorcycle cruising north down the blacktop county road at high speed, its single light cutting through the darkness. The motorcycle zips down the highway. Nat drops his shotgun and fumbles to escape from his load of ducks as he digs in his pocket. Finally freeing his cell phone, he dials Charlie. "How'd you guys do?" Charlie answers on his cell phone.

"Uncle Charlie!" Nat yells into the phone. "We just saw that motorcycle tear by heading north on the county road!"

Chapter 37
React

Charlie and Austin work up the beginnings of a sweat as they enjoy the serenity of the nightfall. Dusk descends and the men walk carefully, in silence through the cornstalks. It's a little over a half mile back to

Charlie's house from their cornfield blind. The mood couldn't be lighter; each man carries fistfuls of bright orange as well as his shotgun. It was an easy jaunt out to the field, but now it's a pleasant chore with a near limit of ducks in hand. Charlie's phone buzzes in his pocket and he grins wider as he sees it's Nat on the line. He answers, "How'd you do?"

He freezes and drops the ducks from his hands and begins to run toward the house. Austin is perplexed. "C'mon! That was Nat. They just saw the motorcycle. We gotta get to Veronica!"

Austin tosses his ducks onto the pile of mallards left by Charlie and sprints ahead through the last rows of corn stalks, into the grass dividing the field and the coulee. Down through the drainage he is not gaining on Charlie, but Charlie slows to yell back, "Load your gun!"

"It's still loaded," Austin shouts back.

The men move as quickly as they can up the slope of the coulee in the descending twilight. The red has disappeared from the sky, and the dark purple tones of the night fall as a shroud. The yard light flickers near the house and draws Charlie's focus as he pushes into his second wind. Onto the two rut trail, Charlie can kick into high gear without fear of tripping in the darkness, the path is clear and he covers the ground quickly, widening the gap between Austin who trails by almost fifty yards now.

Past the stack of bales and a quarter mile across the hayfield to the front yard they move in a rush. Charlie signals Austin silently to hold back. Quietly up the steps to the front porch he moves. He eases the storm door open and flings open the front door, bursting into the living room. Veronica lets loose a blood curdling scream from her position on the couch where she reads a magazine with the local news on television in the background. "Charlie! What on God's green earth are you doing? You scared the bejeezus out of me!"

"Thank God," Charlie gasps. Struggling to regain his breathing, he chokes on the words as he moves to the couch, kneels and wraps an arm around Veronica, shotgun still in his other hand. He wipes sweat from his brow.

"What? What's the matter?" Veronica questions, still panicked, she pats Charlie's back as he holds her.

Veronica flinches again. "Jesus!" She exclaims as Austin pokes through the door, gun at his shoulder, ready to fire.

"I heard a scream." Austin tips the barrel of the gun towards the ceiling. "Sorry about that," Austin pants, out of breath.

"What the hell is going on?" Veronica demands as she pushes Charlie away.

Charlie meets Veronica's eyes. "Nat called. Him and Claude are hunting up on Hakkens' a couple miles north. They said they saw the motorcycle going by on the county blacktop. I thought..."

"I'm fine," Veronica assures.

A collective sigh of relief falls across the room, both men still gasp for air. "Hey, Charlie," Austin speaks quietly. "I suppose I better go get those ducks."

"Just wait for Nat." Charlie halts Austin heading out the door. "He can help you. We won't clean 'em tonight. We'll just gut them and hang 'em overnight."

Austin steps out on the porch to try to cool down, "Sounds good." He leans out to see around the house. "I think they're coming back right now."

Lights turn into the driveway and the truck approaches. "Yeah, that's them."

Chapter 38
He's Got Pluck

"Thanks for helping me pluck all these ducks, Agent Brown," Nat acknowledges as he tosses a handful of feathers in the air.

Nat and Austin each pluck feathers from their third duck of the day. Set up about a hundred yards from the house, they work in what's left of the shade of the trees along the coulee in the warm mid-October Saturday morning. The tall grass along the coulee looks like a truck load of pillows exploded. Feathers are everywhere, and the slightest breeze from the south assists the men by keeping the feathers at bay and out of their faces. "What do we got? Four down, sixteen to go?" Austin asks rhetorically, already knowing the answer, having carefully monitored the situation. He had gravely underestimated the chore when Charlie called him first thing in the morning. The work involved with picking just one duck was something he never imagined, and they each had to do a total of ten. This was going to be a four or five hour job by his estimation.

"Nice and convenient that everyone else is working today. On a Saturday," Nat comments sarcastically. "Thanks again, Agent Brown."

"It's no problem. And, by the way, you can call me Austin. You're like you're Uncle Charlie. He insists on calling me Agent Brown."

"But, aren't you still with the FBI?" Nat puzzles aloud.

Austin laughs. "Yes, technically, but I am just Austin as far as you guys are concerned."

Each plucks his duck in silence for a few minutes. "Nothing like hunting ducks over a cornfield," Nat finally says.

"Yeah, that was something else. Amazing." Austin laughs as he recalls the events in his head. "When Charlie and I first walked from his house across the coulee, I thought, 'what are we even doing out here, man?' There was nothing flying and we were just standing beside a cornfield like a couple stooges. Then boom! Ducks everywhere. Zipping and zooming. The air rushing over their wings...I've never heard anything like it."

"Everything went just perfect," Nat chirps. "Seems like Uncle Charlie's plans never fail."

"I coulda done without the excitement of the motorcycle." Austin makes a sour face. "If Charlie's plan included that, his plans are a little too exciting for me."

"Tell me about it." Nat rolls his eyes. "I dropped my shotgun, fumbling around for the phone to call Charlie. Then, you and I had to go get the ducks you guys dropped in the pitch black. Yeah, too exciting for my blood."

The pair picks in silence for a moment before Nat continues, "You should have seen it. I shot twice, and Grandpa only shot once. Ducks were raining down everywhere. Three shots, fourteen ducks. I have never seen or heard of such a thing."

Austin flips a hand at the pile of ducks they still have to pluck. "Yeah, nice job."

Nat laughs heartily.

"What's the deal with picking them, anyway? Why can't we just cut the breasts out? Or just skin them?"

"Oh, don't let Grandpa hear you say that." Nat holds up the nearly naked mallard he's working on. "You see this breast? This layer of fat? That's where all the flavor is. Grandpa insists that this is the only way to clean ducks." Nat shakes his head. "He always says, 'if you're going to shoot 'em, you're going to clean 'em and cook 'em right." Nat shrugs. "It's hard to argue with him when you taste 'em."

"Yeah," Austin concurs. "I had those leftovers the other night. They were excellent. Delicious."

Conversation quiets and each man works on another duck. It's Nat that interrupts again with a question. "So, what about this Elliot? You guys gonna get him?"

A darkness falls over Austin, like a cloud. His mood flips from the joy of the hunt and the hard work of cleaning the harvested ducks to a cold, serious demeanor. He frowns and picks harder and faster on his duck. "We've kind of hit a dead end."

"What do you mean?" Nat pauses his plucking and holds up a hand. "We saw him last night. Why can't the FBI and law enforcement just swarm in and get him?"

Austin tears at the feathers of the bird. "It's just not that simple. It's not like you see on TV shows. The FBI's primary mission is fighting terrorism now. Like I said, technically I'm still with the FBI, and I'm a one man team hunting this guy, but it's unofficial. It's not like I can call in a chopper and swoop down and get him. It just doesn't work that way." Austin pauses a moment, glancing at Nat. "I'm relying on local law enforcement, your Uncle Charlie, to help me get this guy."

"I don't understand," Nat confesses. "It seems confusing. This guy killed people, and you're the only one really assigned to get him? Doesn't make sense."

"Welcome to government bureaucracy. It's definitely not like movies Hollywood puts out, that's for sure," Austin remarks softly.

They fall silent as they each work on a fresh bird and a few minutes pass. "I'll tell you what," Austin finally offers. "This is a lot more work than I thought it was going to be."

Nat laughs. "You ready for a break?"

Austin grunts an affirmation to the question. "I've been eyeing the backboard." He gives a nod to the driveway and the basketball hoop. "What do you say? We'll finish up these, then take a break and shoot some baskets."

"Sure." Nat grins. "You play ball in school?"

"In junior high school. I'm originally from Cleveland. Believe me, there's a lot of kids that could play ball. Hence, my basketball career ended early."

Nat chuckles. "That's ok. I'll take it easy on ya."

"I can hold my own. Don't get me wrong, I play at the YMCA during lunch sometimes."

"Yeah, like I said. I'll take it easy on ya."

Chapter 39
Driveway Dominance

Swish. Nat sinks an eighteen-foot jump shot effortlessly. The net cracks like a whip and Austin gathers the ball. "Nice shot," Austin remarks casually. "Charlie says you're pretty good."

Nat's face scrunches at the words. Pretty good is quite the understatement, even by Nat's own objective, and fairly humble, estimation. He receives a pass from Austin and launches another shot that is nothing but net. "I guess you'll find out."

There are people that can put the basketball through the hoop, but Nat makes shooting the basketball a piece of performance art. Through thousands of hours on this driveway basketball court, he's refined his shooting skill to a masterpiece. No wasted motion, he's not a high rising jump shooter. That lesson came early from Uncle Charlie. Your legs get tired and you lose accuracy of your shot. It was the tenth commandment of basketball. Larry Bird, the Legend, was the example of this tenet of shooting a basketball.

Nat is a "high arc-er." The ball comes down at such a steep angle that it is sometimes deceptive as it passes through the net. The net might move so minimally, that your brain is not convinced that the ball has gone through the hoop, but believe it. It did. Physics studies have shown that the higher the arc, and the steeper the angle the ball enters the cylinder, the better the chance the ball will pass through hoop. It is a fairly simple ratio based on angles of deflection. Plus, it is just so much more beautiful to see a rainbow of a shot rain down from above and snap that net. In fact, that crack of the net that sounds like the crack of a whip, it is the same principle, the fabric breaking the sound barrier, on a small scale.

Austin gathers the ball and clangs a shot off the rim from four feet. The ball bounces away and Nat hustles to grab it. The late morning sun is warm and bright on the driveway. "Pretty warm for October," Austin notes.

"I see how it is," Nat laughs out loud. "Making excuses already? Sun got in my eyes?"

"I'm just saying."

"I'm just teasing you." Nat tosses the ball to Austin who banks in an eight foot shot from the side. "There you go, but you better learn to talk some trash. At least on this court. That's how we do it." Nat scoops up the ball. "You know, Uncle Charlie can't beat me anymore. Hasn't in a couple years, so don't get discouraged. He was pretty darn good."

Austin is at a loss and answers randomly with a question. "Thanks? For the words of comfort?" as he shrugs his shoulders.

Nat laughs loudly. "You'll be alright. Just keep that attitude. Go ahead. You take it first."

Austin maneuvers to the top of the key and Nat checks the ball to him. "Ball," Nat says softly as he bounces it to him. Austin grabs the ball and moves quickly by Nat who is standing lock-kneed, not ready. Austin is quick, but not quick enough for the youthful Nat. He recovers in time to block the layup attempt by Austin.

"Dang it!" Austin clucks his tongue and pants for air as he gets his own rebound. "Gonna be tougher than I thought. Young. Lanky. Half-a-head taller 'n' me..."

"No mercy." Nat wipes at his nose as he bends his knees and crouches into a defensive position guarding Austin.

Austin dribbles back to the top of the key, fakes left, and spin dribbles right providing an opening to shoot from the right elbow, the right side of the free throw line and the key intersection point. The ball bounces harmlessly off the rim and Nat corrals the rebound. He dribbles the ball casually moving to the top of the key as Austin falls back on defense. "Can we make this interesting?" Nat questions.

"What do you mean?"

Nat dribbles the ball between his legs as he talks at the top of the key. "How about if you beat me, I'll pick the rest of the ducks myself. I win, you do two of every three that are left."

Austin contemplates a second and reaches out a hand and they shake on the wager. "Deal," Austin concurs.

"First to eleven."

"By ones?"

"Yup." Nat picks up his dribble. "Check it and we'll go." He flips the ball to Austin, who just taps the ball back to him.

Nat catches the ball and in one smooth motion, shoots the ball. Swish.

"Shit," Austin grumbles.

It's only the start of Austin's troubles on the court. He can't score. For every shot that he can get launched, half are blocked by Nat or clang off the rim. He misses again and Nat scores, spinning on a matador defensive effort by Austin. Nat blows by and finger-rolls the ball just over the rim. "I guess I'm a little rusty." Austin shrugs sheepishly.

The game ends eleven to one. Austin's lone bucket comes on a layup as a result of Nat deciding to tie his shoe after checking the ball. The men drink from the garden hose and catch their breath. "Don't let me forget to disconnect the hose after we wash out the ducks. I forgot one time during the fall and it froze. Cracked the faucet. Uncle Charlie never let's me forget."

Austin sniffs a laugh as he pants, short of breath. "Yeah, I learned the hard way my first year in Pierre. It gets nice out in late fall and seems like summer, then bang, cold front comes through and goes from sunny and seventy-five degrees in the afternoon to fifteen degrees the next morning. Cost me about a three hundred dollar plumbing bill for that lesson."

"C'mon." Nat walks toward the coulee where the ducks remain. "Let's take a break, each pick another duck, and catch our breath. Then, a rematch."

Austin follows Nat across the yard to the tree line. "You're quite a gentleman, letting the senior citizen recover."

Chapter 40
Rematch

Twenty minutes after the first game on the driveway, and after each almost finishing plucking another duck, the men are back on the court looking a little worse for the wear. Feathers and down stick to their sweaty and bloody hands. Their shirts and hair also reflect the feathery residue from their labors. Neither is concerned with appearances. Another game of basketball is a welcome break from the tedious chore of cleaning all the ducks.

At the top of the key Austin waits for Nat to check him the ball. "Tell you what." Nat holds the ball. "I'm gonna spot you three."

"How about you give me a chance," Austin counters, hands ready for the ball. "I make a basket, any basket, it's three. Your baskets are one."

"Whoa," Nat blanches. "That seems...oh, well. Deal." Nat checks the ball. "It's only five ducks left. I can handle it if I lose."

Austin grabs the ball and fakes. He dribbles to the side of the basket and Nat half-heartedly waves a hand at the ten foot bank shot, which finds its way home. "Three zip!" Austin exclaims excitedly.

"Alright." Nat grins. "You've had your fun, old man."

Nat turns up the defense and scores almost at will from outside, taking a six to three lead. The game rages. Austin is trying to out-muscle the youngster to no avail. Austin flips up a running teardrop that bounces off the back of the rim. In a clumsy attempt to rebound, he bumps Nat, sending him flying into the grass. Focused on the game, the pair is oblivious to the car rolling down the driveway and stopping short of the court. The driver gets out of the car yelling, "What's going on out here? Don't hurt my point guard!"

Austin extends a hand and pulls Nat to his feet as both players look at the man in a green sweat suit. "Coach?" Nat questions. "What are you doing here?" Nat extends his hand and the man grabs it, pulling Nat to his chest with a pat on the back with his free hand.

"I was just up in Fargo, trying to get our next post player to commit. No such luck, yet. The key word being yet. He's six foot nine, but thin. He could be a good one. So, Fargo to here, right in the area, just thought I'd stop in and say 'hi,' so, hello." The coach turns his attention to Austin. He steps forward and extends his hand.

"Sorry," Austin gasps. "Just trying to catch my breath." He reaches out his hand, "I'm FBI Special Agent Austin Brown. I'm friends with his Uncle Charlie." Austin tilts his head toward Nat.

"Coach Vitter. Black Hills State University." The coach pumps Austin's hand as he looks the men up and down. "Wow, you two guys are quite the sight. What's up? Bloody hands? Feathers? Did I catch you at a bad time? Middle of a murder, maybe?" He laughingly picks a feather off of Nat's black t-shirt and lets it float to the ground.

Nat and Austin watch it drift away as they look at each and then their hands, noticing for the first time that they are indeed a mess. Nat says boisterously, "We shot some ducks last night. A whole pile of mallards. Everyone else is working, so Agent Brown and I got stuck with butchering duties. We've been plucking 'em all morning, so we're just taking a break." Nat looks at Austin. "We must look ridiculous."

"Yeah, frighteningly ridiculous," the coach comments wide-eyed. "Charlie's not around? I'd like to talk to both of you real quickly about something, but everyone's working, eh?"

The Coach's shoulders slump a bit. "Well, I'll give you the three-minute pitch and you can talk it over with your uncle and grandpa. Here's the deal. I'd like you to come out for summer school and get acclimated early."

"What do you mean?" Nat's face wrinkles as he considers the question.

Austin pipes up, "Is that like what the college football players do? They graduate in winter, so they go to college early and get in a spring practice?"

The coach points a finger at Austin. "Exactly. You wouldn't have to leave high school early. Just get enrolled for summer school and we'll get you on a weight lifting program. Get you a job, etc." Nat nods in understanding and the coach continues his spiel. "For basketball, we're not quite as aggressive as football. Most of the guys on the team will be there. Mind you, nothing's official, we can't violate NCAA or NAIA rules, but the older guys know the routines. Plenty of pickup games for them to teach you the offense and play with guys, and against guys that have talent the likes of which you haven't seen at the high school level."

Nat listens carefully, ball on his hip. It sounds interesting, but he is stoic as he hears the pitch. "Hmmph," Austin chimes in again. "Sounds pretty cool."

Nat drops the ball and dribbles between his legs effortlessly. He picks up the ball and spins it on his finger, barely even aware that he's doing it as he thinks. Coach Vitter continues, making his final pitch. "The best thing about the summer session is that it gives you an introduction to college life on a much smaller scale than the typical first jolt of a fall semester. You'll be ahead of the hundreds of stupid college freshmen, really just high-schoolers, no offense, Nat." The coach flashes a wink and a grin at Austin and Nat, "Kids away from home for the first time. The summer session gets you indoctrinated into college life with a lot less chaos. We've found it works pretty good."

Nat dribbles the ball again. The coach cocks his head. "Think you might be interested?"

"Yeah," Nat responds after a moment. "What kind of job could I get?"

"There's all kinds. It's the Black Hills! It's Black Hills State University; we got connections that can line you up with some good, nicely compensated work." Coach Vitter winks at Austin. "Listen, you talk it over with Charlie and your grandpa. See what they think."

The coach moves to the car. "I got some driving to do, so I'd better get rolling, but come here. I got some gear for you."

Austin and Nat immediately gravitate to the car upon hearing "gear." Coach Vitter pops the trunk of his Ford Taurus with the remote. "Here's some t-shirts. Large or medium?"

"Gimme large." Nat shrugs.

The coach hands over a dozen t-shirts of various styles and colors sporting the BHSU Yellow Jacket logo. "And you, Mr. FBI? What size? You want a couple?"

Austin looks to Nat as if he needs permission. Nat offers a shrugging nod. "Sure. Just give me a couple. Large, please."

The coach hands over the t-shirts and flashes a smile akin to Santa at Christmas. "Hold on," he exclaims breathlessly. "I almost forgot." He digs through another box in the trunk. He extracts a dark green, shiny, nylon warm up jacket. "Here's some leisure wear for you."

"Is that a team warm up jacket? Cool!" Nat bristles with excitement. He shoves his stack of t-shirts into Austin's arms. "Can I see it?"

"Sure, it's yours." The coach flips the jacket around and "CHASING WOLF" is lettered across the shoulders.

Nat accepts the jacket and tries it on, smoothing out the sleeves. He eyes Austin. "Pretty cool, huh?"

Austin edges forward, peering into the trunk. "That is awesome. You don't have something like that in there that says 'BROWN' on the back, do you?" He smiles mischievously at the coach.

The coach cackles a laugh. "Make a donation to Yellow Jacket athletics, and we can see what happens. Listen, guys, I gotta go. Get back to your game...or whatever it is you're doing. Talk it over with Charlie and Claude. Love to get you an early start."

The coach cordially shakes Austin's hand and then Nat's, pulling him in for a hug. "Nice to meet you, FBI. See you, Nat."

The coach is in the car and headed down the driveway and Nat and Austin toss a wave his way. Nat turns to Austin. "What'd you say we throw these shirts inside? We still gotta settle who gets to clean the rest of the ducks."

Chapter 41
Editorial

Charlie's House

"You got a minute, Grandpa?" Nat questions, exiting his room.

Claude is perched on a seat at the kitchen table. He looks up from his checkbook over the top of his reading glasses. "Sure. What's up?"

Nat moves to the kitchen table, pulls out a chair and has a seat. He glances to his grandfather and then to his hands folded in front of him on the wooden surface. "I was just thinkin'."

"I hope you didn't pull something," Claude grimaces at his weak attempt at humor, as he brushes his glasses from his face.

Undeterred, Nat grins. "I'm not sure I like being an Indian...I mean I don't understand it."

Claude is caught a bit off guard by the statement and his expression reflects his own thoughts. "You know what? I know exactly what you mean."

"I don't want to sound ungrateful. " Nat's face pinches and he shifts uncomfortably in his chair. "I just don't...with the opportunity to leave Sisseton and go early to college, I thought I'd feel scared or sad, or something. I just want to go. The Reservation is depressing. No offense."

Claude sets his glasses aside on the table and crosses his arms. "Why would I be offended? You and ninety-nine out of one hundred Indians probably feel the same way. You're lucky, you got this opportunity, and the last thing Charlie and I want for you is to feel obligated to say here with us."

Nat relaxes. His whole speech he had prepared to justify going early to Black Hills State was not needed. He had worried a little that his uncle and grandfather would feel slighted, abandoned, but now he feels assured. Claude frowns. "I never want you to feel like you are obligated by your heredity. You are an American. You have freedom. You can define who you are. Don't let the Reservation define you."

"Thanks, Grandpa," Nat breathes the words softly. "I struggle. I don't know my place in the world. Native, Indian, all these labels."

"You're not the first to bear that burden...won't be the last." Claude looks away from his grandson a moment, proud of this boy becoming a man. "It's a failed experiment," he announces with authority. "If I was King for a day, I would erase all the treaties, all the Federal Government's trust requirements, and us Indians designated as wards of the state. It's a crime what's happened. If only we had leaders that would make decisions in good conscience and not just politically motivated, we could right the ship."

Nat cocks his head and looks at his grandfather quizzically. "What are you saying?"

"Well," Claude purses his lips and thinks a moment. "It's simple to me. They took our pride. A person, an Indian has nothing if you don't have pride. The government set us aside. Made us 'special.' We're Americans! Just give us that back!" Claude's emotions rise, but he puts them in check quickly. "The first step is to stop what we're doing. It's not working. If you've heard it once, you've heard it a thousand times. The definition of insanity is doing the same thing over and over and expecting different results." Claude's head shakes and his hands go up in question. "Does the Reservation resemble insanity? I'll answer my own question, absolutely!"

Nat looks away from his grandfather. He rubs his chin and looks back, eyes locking with his grandpa. "So what now? I mean...what about you? What about Uncle Charlie? Why are you guys still on the reservation?"

"I can only speak for myself, but I've always loved 'home.' I saw the jungle in Vietnam. I saw other places in the military, but I like to hunt and fish. This place is for me. I don't need the Reservation, but I need the Coteau. As for your Uncle Charlie, I always feared that he only stayed to take care of me and your grandma. I suspect he thought he could give back to the people with his job in law enforcement. But, he made his decision. He served in the military. He saw the desert in Iraq and chose to come home. Again it's a choice. Many of our brothers and the sisters on the rez have no choice. They've started their life with a handicap...just being Indian." Claude takes a deep breath, his cheeks expand, and he breathes out. "Reservations are the bane of the Indian in my opinion. If I could abolish them now, I would."

Nat nods in agreement. "Will it ever change?"

"Not in my lifetime." Claude frowns. "I always hope and pray that it will, and I remain optimistic. Nothing lasts forever. Ashes to ashes, dust to dust, they say."

"I'm going, Grandpa. I'm going to college as soon as I can and I don't want to come back to the reservation."

"I had the military, you have basketball. I'm very proud of you. You have a gift. Use it."

"I won't let you down, Grandpa. I just feel sorry for those that have no choice but to stay. I hope you are right, that someday, everyone is just an 'American.'"

"Don't hold your breath." Claude frowns. "All those politicians on the East Coast love the romanticized image of Indians. Nope, one can only hope for the best, but prepare for the worst." He beams as he looks across the table at his grandson. "You're going to do great. You got the right attitude, plus you have your mom's penchant for critical thinking as you demonstrated by bringing up this subject. I'm very proud of you, Nathaniel Chasing Wolf."

Chapter 42
Eavesdropper

Sisseton, South Dakota

The bingo hall is part of the Dakota Connection Casino, restaurant, and truck stop. Travelers along Interstate 29 can take a break on the east edge of Sisseton, have a bite to eat, get some fuel, drop a dollar or two into a slot machine, and hope to strike it rich. The local population frequents the bingo hall with an inclination towards socializing, rather than a get-rich-quick gamble. The Sisseton-Wahpeton Sioux Tribe owns and manages the business on the reservation. It is an important employment center for an isolated Indian tribe. One of those employees is a part time bingo caller and tribal member Claude LeBeau. More of a motivation to get out of the house than anything else, Claude enjoys a couple shifts a week calling numbers in the bingo parlor where most of the players are women in his peer group. "G-47," Claude announces through his microphone, and the letter and number are repeated, "G-47."

There is a commotion in the back of the bingo hall. "Did I hear someone say 'Bingo?' Yes, Bingo! Way in the back! Come on up and verify."

The bingo game manager verifies the winning card along with Claude. "It's a good Bingo. We're going to take a five minute break. Get your new cards and be back. Five minutes!"

The mid-Saturday afternoon crowd is a group of the usual retirees killing some time, playing for minimum pots of money. They shuffle to get their new game cards and Claude ducks into the employees-only door to use the rest room. The overhead sound system plays "Don't Make Me" by Blake Shelton just at the prescribed volume of the Casino management company, soft, but not too soft.

Passing the Casino Manager's office marked by a sign on the door indicating "COURTNEY GERMAN" he hears the familiar voice of his son. The partially opened door to Courtney's office allows the voices inside to escape, muffled, but audible. Claude delays his trip to the restroom and listens undetected outside the door.

Inside her office, Courtney German sits behind her desk. Charlie, in his uniform, stands with thumbs in his utility belt. He examines the wall behind Courtney. She displays her undergraduate and masters degrees, nicely framed with maroon and gold matting, products of the University of Minnesota. She also displays a framed and matted certificate and photo from Pillsbury Corporation, thanking her for her service.

Courtney is as beautiful as ever. The thirty two year old woman sports perfectly coiffed, long, straight black hair to the middle of her back. She looks impeccable in her professional pant suit. Charlie's eyes drift from the walls to the beautiful lady in front of him. She seems out of place in Charlie's mind. She is dressed for the board rooms of a Wall Street investment firm. Charlie remembers the situation; she probably would be on Wall Street if she wasn't a generous and loving daughter, home to take care of a mother stricken with Alzheimer's.

The office is dark. Windowless. Typical of casino construction. "Have you told Brittney?" Charlie asks softly, his eyes sympathetic. For Charlie, he always sees Courtney the same, she is a Native American version of Angie Harmon, the beautiful television star.

Courtney nods. "I've finally talked to her about it."

"How'd it go?"

"She's a sharp girl. She understands...life. It doesn't always work out the way you imagine. She's already seen it. The divorce. Moving from Minneapolis to Sisseton. Watching her grandmother waste away. Now Courtney's seen her best friend abandoned by her family. Telling her about you was nothing."

"She's going to have to hear it in court all over again." Charlie frowns. "Is she going to be ok? Listening to me talk about it in front of the judge and other strangers?"

"Don't worry, Charlie. She understands things. She had a dad, that didn't work out. Now, you're in the picture. It's going to take some time."

"Did she say anything? Does she want anything to do with me?" Charlie winces at his own questions. "I guess, I should be asking you. Do you want me to be a part of her life and your life?"

"I left it up to her. I told her I think we should just take things slow. Get settled in with her new foster-sister and worry about all this a little later. At her pace. If she wants to get to know her biological father, it's up to her."

Claude strains to listen in the hallway. The words buckle his knees. "Biological father?" The phrase rattles in his head.

Courtney stands and moves to the front of her desk, closer to Charlie. She sits on the edge of her desk. Her tailored clothing is perfect. Her shirt collar is modestly buttoned to her neck, but remains open enough to display a beautiful turquoise necklace in the shape of a turtle. Charlie eyes her shoes. She wears one inch heels that appear to be European and expensive. "Charlie," she folds her hands in her lap. "I can't thank you enough. For all you've done and are doing. I'm sorry things couldn't be different." Courtney smiles painfully, she nods to the ring on Charlie's finger and Charlie glances down at his hand in realization. "I've put in good words with Brittney for you. She'll come around. At least I hope so. We could use a good man in our lives." The comment draws a smile to Charlie's lips. "You know how little girls are...well, maybe you don't know exactly, but they can be a little difficult. And this situation with Haley...well, what can I say?" Her voice trails off, the melancholy in her tone edges through.

Charlie pushes off the wall and approaches Courtney. He extends his arms. "Don't worry. We may return to some normalcy soon enough."

Courtney stands and hugs Charlie. "Starting after the hearing on Monday. I look forward to it. Normalcy. I'll see you there."

Charlie chuckles to himself, wondering if she is referring to seeing him in normalcy or at the courthouse. "Yup. I'll see you there. I gotta go."

Charlie breaks free from the hug and heads to the door. "Bye," Charlie waves.

"Goodbye."

In the hallway, Claude is in full panic mode as he absorbs the information, but now Charlie is heading straight toward him and is going to discover that he's been spying on him. Claude bounds down the hall. He ducks into the family restroom and clicks the lock on the door. Charlie exits Courtney's office and heads the opposite direction, unaware of Claude's eavesdropping.

Chapter 43
Hearing

Roberts County Courthouse – Sisseton, South Dakota

The hearing is over and judgment is passed. The Honorable Doris Fetteberg taps her gavel on the desk and concludes the session. Courtney hugs Haley and is joined in the hug by Brittney as everyone stands. Courtney has successfully petitioned for full custody of Haley. The social services representative, Dee, approaches the bench and shakes the judge's hand before moving to join the hug with Courtney. It is a successful outcome for all involved, as Judge Fetteberg noted in her statement, "Today is what seems like a rare day in family court where everyone is smiling." Fetteberg in her formal black robe, John Lennon-type round, wire glasses with her hair pulled tightly into a bun at the back of her head, looks more like a middle-aged nun than a judge. She smiles to herself as she stows her papers away in her leather valise, her day is over, at least in the courtroom anyway.

Charlie watches the celebration of the closed hearing from a back bench in the far corner of the courtroom. His eyes meet the judge's, and they exchange a nod. He waves to Courtney. She looks at him and mouths the words, "Thank you," as he exits through a hallway near the judge's chambers. Hoping to avoid attention, Charlie ducks out the side exit of the courthouse. He rounds the corner of the courthouse headed to his BIA Police Tahoe parked on Maple Street, just a block east off Sisseton's central business district.

Charlie spots Claude leaning against his Tahoe. "Dad? Why are you here? Is something wrong?"

"You tell me," Claude orders brusquely as he stands up straight, arms folded.

"Just giving some testimony at a hearing," Charlie replies.

"I don't think so. Was Courtney German in there?"

"If you need to know, yes. I was testifying on her behalf. She was seeking custody as a foster parent for Haley Hopkins." Claude's eyes lock onto Charlie's as he listens. Charlie notes the intense expression of his father. "What's wrong?"

"I overheard you talking to Courtney. The other day at the Casino."

"What? What are you talking about?" Charlie is confused. "You were eavesdropping?"

"Tell the truth, Charlie. Don't you dare lie to me. Are you that girl's father?"

Charlie looks around, but the street is empty. He pushes close to Claude, pinning him against the Tahoe with one hand on the vehicle, his other hand wags a finger in his face. "Dad, that is not true," his voice is calm but scolding. "I do need to talk to you about something, but this isn't the time or place." Charlie backs away.

Courtney exits the front of the courthouse fifty yards away with Haley and Brittney in tow. The girls are bundles of energy, skipping and circling Courtney like satellites in her orbit. Charlie and Claude watch the family as they move closer heading to their car. At twenty five yards away, Courtney sees Charlie and waves as she opens the door to her minivan and loads the girls in the back.

Claude sighs and relaxes against the vehicle. He sees the resemblance. "It's not the Hopkins girl. It's Courtney's daughter." His voice is a whisper.

Charlie holds a finger to his lips. Claude pleads with his son, "Why didn't you tell me? Does Veronica know?"

"Dad, this isn't the time or place."

"My God."

Charlie puts up his hands in surrender, "Fine. I just found out. I told Veronica as soon as I knew. Nobody is trying to keep secrets. Courtney didn't know until a couple of years ago. There was a medical emergency and testing revealed that her husband wasn't Brittney's father. It could only have been me."

"I can see the resemblance," Claude states matter-of-factly. "You just found out now?"

"There was no reason that I should know. She had her family. I only found out working the Hopkins case, and only because of Courtney's Alzheimer's-ridden mother."

Claude turns away from Charlie. He is confused as he watches Courtney and her girls drive away. Charlie continues, "Are you even listening? Her mother blurted it out. Courtney came clean and filled me in on the details."

Claude turns back to his son, beaming. He hugs Charlie. "This is good news, Charlie! I have a granddaughter!"

Charlie reluctantly accepts the hug. He is less than thrilled at the public display. "Yeah," he replies with all the excitement of man undergoing a root canal.

Chapter 44
Extra! Extra!

Charlie's House

Supper is over and the dishes put away. In their bedroom, Charlie watches Veronica extract a clean pair of pajamas from her dresser drawer and head to the bathroom. "You're going to bed?" Charlie questions. "It's barely 7:30."

"I'm exhausted," Veronica huffs as she disappears behind the closing door of the master bath.

"I'm going to go watch TV," Charlie raises his voice to be heard through the closed door.

"Ok," the muffled response comes from the other side of the door.

The door opens and Veronica emerges in her pajamas. A puzzled Charlie looks at Veronica curiously. "That was fast."

"I'm tired," Veronica shrugs. She reaches up and kisses Charlie.

She climbs into bed. "I need to tell you something," Charlie says meekly.

"What is it? Is it serious?" Veronica tenses at Charlie's tone.

"You know I had to testify at the hearing today."

Yeah."

Charlie heaves a sigh. "Dad knows about Brittney and Courtney." Veronica cocks her head not fully understanding.

Charlie sits on the edge of the bed and continues, "Apparently he overheard me and Courtney this weekend discussing the hearing. He was calling bingo and I stopped by the casino to talk to Courtney about my testimony. He was on break or something and overheard our conversation." Charlie looks toward the door and rolls his eyes, directed at Claude out in the living room. "So, I come out of the courthouse and guess who's leaning up against my vehicle."

"No. Claude?"

"Yeah! He confronts me right out on the street. And get this. He thought I was the father of the Hopkins girl that we were having the hearing for. He apparently couldn't hear our conversation so well when he was listening in. He just heard I was testifying at the hearing on Courtney's behalf as a foster parent, but was confused about the girls."

Veronica laughs, throwing her head back. "That is hilarious. He must have been in a tizzy."

Charlie laughs now, "Tizzy? Really? You English majors and your words. Let's just say he was pretty upset." Charlie pauses and feverishly shakes his head. "Then, here comes Courtney and the two girls out the front entrance of the courthouse. They get closer and closer. Claude does a double-take and realizes that it's Courtney's daughter that is the one...you know. He says he can see the resemblance. Suddenly he's all happy and hugging me out on the street. 'I have a granddaughter!' He's all excited. Then he goes quiet. He's all concerned about whether you know or not."

Veronica laughs again. "Oh. How cute. He's concerned about me." She reaches for Charlie's hand and entwines his fingers in hers.

"Anyhoo, I just wanted you to know." Charlie frowns. "The word's out. He can't keep a secret, so you might as well have published it on the front page of your paper." Charlie puts his free hand to his mouth and calls out, "Extra! Extra! Read all about the secret child!"

Veronica giggles. "Stop it. Don't worry about it. We still got our other secret." Veronica pats her belly with Charlie's hand in hers.

Charlie leans down and kisses her. "Oh well, now you know." He stands, "I'm going to watch some football. Good night."

"Night."

Veronica falls asleep quickly.

*   *   *

Two blocks from Sisseton's central business district, under the dimly lit street of a residential area, Elliot parks his motorcycle. It's a short walk in the cool night air to the Roberts County Standard Newspaper Office on Veterans Avenue. Tucked in the shadows across the street from the newspaper office, Elliot peers through the storefront window. He observes the dark haired woman still hunched over her computer well after 10:30 at night. Her back is to the windows and the front of the store.

Elliot approaches the door of the newspaper office, his black leather jacket, chaps, and black helmet blend him into the shadows of the night. He opens the door and it gongs an alert. The woman at the desk holds up a hand for a moment, and then continues to type, finishing her thought without looking up. "I'm sorry," she says without turning around. "That door is supposed to be locked. We're closed."

"Veronica?" Elliot questions in a near whisper, the helmet muffling his voice.

Kelli turns at the confusing question; she begins to smile at the mistaken identity. As her chair turns, her smiles twists into a fearful frown and she throws her hands up in defense as she looks down the barrel of a pistol. Elliot fires the weapon. The bullet passes through Kelli's hand, then her skull, finally lodging in the computer screen. A spray of misted blood coats everything in the bullet's trail.

"What the fuck? Who is this?" Elliot questions with a shout, his voice muted by motorcycle helmet. A confused Elliot backs away from the body, moving toward the utility closet, still determined to execute his plan. Opening the closet door, he spies the natural gas pipe to the furnace. He smashes his heavy leather boot down on the metal pipe until it finally gives way with a hiss.

Elliot moves to the front windows as he pulls a small candle and a lighter from his pocket. He lights the candle and places it on the window ledge as he exits. He pulls the door tightly shut behind him and breaks into a jog down the empty street. He puts a block and a half behind him and his motorcycle is in sight before the explosion rips through the darkness. He can see the flickering lights reflected on the buildings around him. He doesn't turn to look. He knows his mission for the night is complete.

Mounting his motorcycle, he flips the switch and the bike roars to life between his legs with a deafening growl, and his crotch-rocket shoots him off into the inky-black darkness.

*   *   *

Veronica's eyes snap open in the darkness and she cries out, "Kelli!"

In the living room, Charlie looks over his shoulder back to the bedroom. "Did you hear that?" Charlie questions as he mutes the college football game on the television.

"No, hear what?" Claude responds, annoyed at the interruption as he reads his newspaper.

In the bedroom, Veronica sits up in bed, still in the fog of her dream. "Charlie!"

"Veronica!" Charlie shouts, tossing the remote control onto the couch and bolting to the bedroom.

Bursting through the door, Charlie flips on the light to find Veronica trembling as she sits straight up in bed. She struggles to catch her breath. Charlie looks around the room and sees no danger. He kneels next to the bed, wrapping his arms around his wife. "It's ok. You just had a bad dream." He pats her back, comforting the shivering woman.

Veronica cries, body shaking in sobs. "Shhh. It's ok," Charlie pleads.

Claude moves into the doorway and Nat slides in behind him. "What's going on?" Claude questions.

Charlie rocks the vulnerable woman, trying to shield her from his uncle and nephew. "Just a nightmare. Go back to the TV."

Veronica's chest heaves as her breathing remains a chore. Claude and Nat move back to the living room and Charlie kicks the door closed. "Kelli. Call Kelli," Veronica insists between gulps of air. "I saw Elliot at the office. Get Kelli on the phone."

"What? In your dream?"

"Just call her!" Veronica insists.

Charlie plucks his cell phone from his shirt pocket. He scrolls through his phone and cringes. "I don't have her number."

"Use my phone!" Veronica orders.

Charlie grabs Veronica's phone from the nightstand and dials the number. "It's ringing," he announces with a whisper.

"Hey, Kelli, this is Charlie. Veronica wanted me to give you a call. Are you still at the office?" Charlie nods to Veronica. "You are? Ok then. Why don't…"

Veronica rips the phone from Charlie's' hand, leaving Charlie positioned with a ghost phone at his ear, stunned at his wife's reaction.

"Hello, Kelli? This is Veronica. Just go home. You've been working too hard. Call it a night. Be careful though." She listens to Kelli. "Ok. Ok. Call me when you get home safe."

Veronica hands the phone to Charlie. He looks at it, confused; he puts the phone to his ear. "Bye, Kelli."

"Charlie?" He hears on the other end. "What's going on?"

Charlie speaks quietly into the phone, "Um, sorry, Kelli. Veronica had a bad dream." Veronica glares at Charlie. "Ok, everything is fine. She'll see you tomorrow. Bye."

The fog of the dream has lifted and Veronica shakes her head as she calms down. "It was so real, Charlie. I can't believe it."

"You want me to go to town and make sure she gets home safely?"

"Could you please?" Veronica bats her eyelashes pleadingly.

Charlie kisses her on the forehead. "Sure. No problem. I'll be right back."

Chapter 45
Repatriation

Veblen, South Dakota

Elliot had debated whether to venture out in daylight for awhile, but his foolish argument ended abruptly with the realization he was a walking dead man. There was nothing to lose. Getting caught was not an issue. He rolled out on his motorcycle, self-conscious of the garden spade strapped to his bike that he had stolen the night before.

* * *

The Kirschner Ranch, just a few miles south of Veblen, is hallowed ground for Elliot. The old Kirschner Ranch gravel pit looked the same now as it did over thirty years ago. It was like a time capsule. Apparently the vein of sand and gravel the pit provided had run out about that time. No efforts to reclaim the disturbed ground have been made. Mounds of topsoil, large cobble stones, and spoil piles from screening gravel dot the three acre plot. Elliot orients himself to the gravel pit, going back to that night...the night he made his first kill. He thought it was going to be more difficult to find the location of her shallow grave, and he is up for the challenge. However, he is disappointed to find the location so quickly. His mood was already black. The dusty ride on the gravel road has put a gritty coat on his beautiful motorcycle, and he fears to inspect the chassis further, worried about the nicks from the gravel he had heard ticking off the motorcycle as he cruised down the unpaved, county road.

Never mind, he is focused on the task at hand, a recovery operation of sorts. He is digging for the body of Shanice.

*   *   *

It is a warm October day and Elliot quickly works up a sweat and, along with his constant shortness of breath now, this demands a break. Sticking the shovel in the ground he walks to the edge of the deepest part of the pit. A flurry of wings and quacking erupts below him. "Jesus Christ!" he calls out as a hundred mallards explode from the scant pond of water at the bottom of the pit.

Elliot grips his chest as his heart pounds and he gasps for air. He can't help but smile at his fright as the flock of ducks gathers altitude, formation shifting over and over in the air as the birds make their getaway. He wonders how in the world the ducks weren't frightened by the roar of the motorcycle when pulled up. No matter, he can laugh now that his heart hadn't exploded in his chest, and he does laugh. First a chuckle, then a full riotous, belly laugh bursts from his diaphragm until he doubles over in a coughing spell. How is life so ridiculous, he wonders, as he tries to regain his breath.

He knows his time on earth is diminishing quickly. That is his motivation today. This afternoon was an inconsistency in his body of work. Shanice is his only victim he hasn't publicly displayed. Empathetic thoughts of a cold-blooded murderer bounce through his head as the shovels-full of rocky soil are cleared away. The incongruity of murder and empathy rattle in his head. What message does this send? Exposing the bones, and eventually, somebody finding them would bring closure to Shanice's family, but that's not his motivation. This was the only body he hadn't officially tallied in his ledger. This would balance his books as far as he was concerned.

His mood is light. The scare put into his body by the flushing flock of ducks had shot him full of adrenaline and the thought of completing this task brought him to as near of a state of giddiness he has had since he could recall. This is it. This is the final chapter. He laughs out loud at the thought of NAGPRA. The Native American Graves Protection and Repatriation Act is a Federal law that focuses on returning funerary objects of Native Americans, particularly those in museums, to their origins. The law also comes into play when construction occurs in the traditional locations of Native American Tribes. When graves are disturbed in earth moving projects, experts and historically associated Tribes are called into make determinations on the disposition of the remains.

Elliot laughs at the confusion this scenario would bring to government officials. Technically this is a Native American grave. His thoughts are interrupted when the spade of the shovel crunches against something obviously not a stone. The excavation had already taken longer than he planned, but he slows down now. He carefully exposes the skeleton the best he can with his only rudimentary tool, the shovel. The sun makes its final rush to the horizon. "Forty five minutes of daylight," Elliot comments aloud as he inspects the western sky. "That's enough."

Shanice's skull is exposed; soil clings to the remains, filling every crevice. Elliot pushes the spade into the ground next to the brown-stained cranium bone. The unblinking eye sockets stare at him. Throwing his leather work gloves to the side he reaches for his ear. He removes two small diamond earrings from his right ear. His trophies. They are returning to their rightful owner. Elliot laughs to himself again...at his own pain. He had only re-pierced his ears a few days ago to reinsert his trophies after not having earrings in them for twenty five years. His earlobe hurts. He can't take much discomfort anymore. His state of health seems to exacerbate any irritation. "Not much longer," Elliot says to himself.

He frowns for a moment, but a smile quickly returns to his face. He drops the two small earrings next to the skull, one on each side, into the exposed grave. He grasps the handle of the shovel for a moment, but lets it drop and waves his hand at it. "I don't need that," he laughs. He shuffles to his motorcycle as he watches the sun begin to set. Scooping up the helmet from the seat of the bike, he mounts the bike and holds the helmet on his lap as he watches the sky turn purple, and the sun disappears behind the Coteau. With a quick glance to the gravesite, all he can see is the handle of the shovel in the weeds. He dons his helmet and buckles it in place.

He has another appointment and it is perfectly timed for dusk and darkness.

Chapter 46
Night Watch

On the gravel township road, Elliot kills the engine on his motorcycle as puts the kickstand down and dismounts the Ducati. Still a half hour from total darkness, he begins his walk across the harvested cornfield. He works the action on his pistol, inserting .45 caliber round into the chamber of the semiautomatic Remington pistol. He eases the hammer down and checks the safety. He walks with his helmet on, face shield up. Another five minutes he will have to don his night vision glasses, but he can manage trudging down the flat, straight, combined rows of corn for a little while more. This is the Hakken's cornfield, the same field Claude and Nat had hunted a few nights before. Tonight, Elliot hikes casually through the leaves and stalks of dried corn plants, shattered by the combine. He is in no hurry. He prefers not to work up a sweat. He has cooled down from his earlier excavation activities, and consciously takes his time strolling through field.

One mile down, one more mile to go. Elliot stops and fixes his night vision scope over his helmet. He clicks on the switch and the batteries wine as electronics charge and suddenly he can see the landscape, everything has a green tinge. His range of vision is only about forty yards and he continues to walk. The breeze picks up. It is only the slightest north wind at his back as he walks south. His destination, Charlie LeBeau's house.

Twenty five minutes later Elliot sits on a downed tree at the bottom of the coulee a hundred yards or so from the house. Now it is just a waiting game. When the lights are all out, he will take care of his nemesis once and for all. The plan had been originally to attack his aggressors directly. The idea had eventually morphed into what seemed like a much crueler, meaningful revenge. Step one was complete. Agent Brown's wife was dead. Brown would forever live with the memory of the Deer Slayer. Elliot had hated the nickname at first, but now he embraced it. It seemed powerful. It had roots in what seemed like its own mythology, a mythology he had wished he had recorded. Early on he had contemplated keeping a journal, but the fear of being discovered had always deterred him. Now, facing his mortality, he wished he had a written history. No, his legacy would be planted in the minds of others as memories of pain and suffering.

Clicking off the night vision scope he sits in the darkness staring at the LeBeau residence. At seven-thirty lights appear at the end of the driveway, turning from the county road. In a moment the vehicle is parked in the drive way. The yard light illuminates Charlie's BIA Tahoe. Charlie exits the vehicle and strolls to the house, up the stairs onto the porch, pulling the door open. He pauses, peering into the darkness, a quick scan for any threat, before disappearing behind the door.

Elliot turns his attention to the yard light. That needs to be eliminated for an approach, he ponders the matter, but his thoughts on that issue are cut short, interrupted by a low growl. He readjusts his night vision goggles a dog twenty-five yards away, downwind, in an opening along the edge of the grass. Hair bristling, teeth bared, the dog stares at him as it continues to growl.

"A dog," Elliot whispers aloud. He hasn't planned for this. He shifts his position, moving to a kneeling position next to the log on which he had been sitting.

The movement sets the dog off in a howl and a series of barks. The dog holds its position, but continues to stare at Elliot and periodically bark. Steadily punctuating the night every twenty seconds or so, the dog barks.

Elliot is uncomfortable. The disturbance by the dog is going to draw attention. Five minutes later the front door opens and Charlie is on the porch peering into the darkness. He looks in the direction of the barking dog, directly in line with Elliot stationed at the bottom of the coulee. "Zero!" Charlie calls out into the night, followed by a shrill whistle. "Here, boy!"

The barking stops. There is no way Charlie can see Elliot, but it is enough for Elliot to abandon the plan. Nat would be safe for tonight. Nat was and is the target. In Elliot's mind, the most devastating loss would be Nat. He vividly remembered the basketball success Nat had enjoyed. He remembered seeing Charlie's pride in his nephew. Nat was the last vestige of Charlie's sister. Yes, killing Nat would be the legacy of pain in Charlie's life that Elliot desired.

Not tonight though. Charlie closes the door disappearing back into the house. The barking resumes moments after the door closes. Elliot stands and retraces his steps back through the bottom of the coulee and into the cornfield. Two hundred yards from the coulee the barking ceases. "Yard light and dog," he mutters aloud. "How do I take care of them?" He thinks as he walks, his mind mulling over options.

*　　*　　*

Inside Charlie's house, Veronica warms a plate of leftover rotisserie chicken from Teal's Market. Charlie returns from his foray outside to investigate the barking dog. He sits at the table, collapsing into the chair. "That's weird." Veronica looks to Charlie. "We got a guard dog out there?"

"Annoying is what it is," Charlie grumbles. "This better not be the new trend, barking at all hours of the night."

Veronica laughs. "Don't be such a grump. Maybe he's just hungry. I'll toss some food out later."

Charlie yawns. "I know. I'm just tired. It's probably nothing."

Chapter 47
Lunch Break

BIA Police Headquarters – Sisseton, South Dakota

Charlie is signing out at the board when Skip sidles up to him. "Where you going?"

"Hmm? Oh." Charlie is already thinking about something to eat. He caps the marker. "Just going home for lunch. You? You going someplace?"

"I'm signing out for the rest of the day. Dentist."

"Have fun," Charlie says wryly.

"Hey, I hate to bug you." Skip grabs the marker and signs out on the white board. He replaces the cap and sets the marker down. "But, did you ever get a hold of Titus?"

"Shoot!" Charlie chews on the word in disgust with himself. "I keep forgetting. I'll call him as soon as I get home. I'm starving."

Skip taps Charlie's belly. "I can see you're starving." He chuckles. "Thanks. I appreciate you calling him. Let me know what he wants."

*　　*　　*

Charlie's BIA police unit, the new model Chevy Tahoe, pulls into his driveway. He silences the radio, prematurely ending Cheap Tricks' song "I Want You to Want Me." Movement along the tree line on the edge of the coulee catches his peripheral vision. It is the dog. Charlie gets a view of the beast from inside the cab of his truck. He pulls out the binoculars he has stashed under his seat and gets an up close and personal view of the mongrel. The dog is medium-sized, about the size of a coyote. It appears to be quite the mix of breeds including boxer, lab and most dominantly, shepherd giving it a distinct coyote look. It works the tree line, nose to the ground, stopping to gaze at Charlie inside the Tahoe, but unafraid of the vehicle. Charlie gets a good look at the dog with his optics as it stares directly at him. One of the dog's eyes has a dark splotch of fur around it. It looks like a black eye. "He's got a shiner," Charlie murmurs aloud.

Charlie stows the binoculars and exits the vehicle. His stomach grumbles, urging him to get inside and find lunch. Inside the house, Charlie sheds his jacket and tosses it on the couch; he unhooks his utility belt and drapes it across the recliner.

"What were you just sitting out in the vehicle for?" Claude questions from the kitchen as he puts the finishing touch on a sandwich and moves to the dining room table.

"I was just looking at the dog. He's back hanging around the yard."

"You mean 'Zero?'"

"I thought we talked about holding off on naming him." Charlie moves into the kitchen. "Besides, I think 'Shiner' is a better name." He

132

points to his eye. "He's got a patch of fur around one eye that makes him look like he's got a black eye."

Claude coughs a laugh between bites. "I like it." He points to the fridge. "The chicken's good for a sandwich."

"Yeah, sounds great." Charlie is looking at his phone, scrolling through contacts. "I gotta make a call first."

Charlie puts the phone to his ear. He grabs a glass from the cupboard and fills it with water from the kitchen faucet as he stands over the sink. He takes a sip, swallows, and is interrupted by a "hello" on the other end of the phone.

Charlie coughs. "Titus, pardon my cough. This is Charlie LeBeau. Sorry I'm so late getting back to you."

Charlie listens for a moment, staring straight ahead, frozen. The glass slips from his hand, crashing down into the sink, breaking in half. "Jesus Christ!" Claude hollers, his voice muffled by a full bite of sandwich. He grips his chest, stands, and glares at Charlie.

Charlie turns to his father with a hand in the air, trying to provide calm to the situation, and mouthing the words, "I'm sorry," as he listens intently on the phone, eyes ever-widening.

"I'm sorry, Titus. Did you just say you saw someone push a motorcycle into that boarded-up house? Earlier this week?"

Charlie listens. "Mmm-hmm. This was a week ago, you said. Mmm-hmm. And you have seen him several times since?"

Charlie is shaking. The phone in his hand trembles and he struggles to keep his voice calm. "Don't do anything," he orders. "Stay in your house. I will be there this afternoon. With my friend from the FBI. We will be in street clothes and a regular, unmarked vehicle. Understand? Just stay in your house."

Charlie listens. "Ok. Good. Thanks. We'll see you in a bit."

Charlie has trouble pushing the button on his phone to end the call, he's shaking with excitement. His eyes are like saucers as he looks to his dad seated back at the table with his sandwich. "I'm pretty sure the Deer Slayer is holed up in a boarded-up house in Veblen."

Chapter 48
Covert Ops

Austin's House – Sisseton, South Dakota

Austin sits at his kitchen table drinking coffee and reading the newspaper. His dirty dishes from lunch are pushed to the far side of the table to make room for the folded newspaper in front of him. Engrossed in the news article and enjoying the midday sun in the kitchen alcove, he doesn't hear Charlie leap up on the front porch, but a woodpecker-like wrapping on the door quickly gets his full attention. Before he can react, Charlie is in the house moving through the living room at jog. "Hey!" Austin calls out a welcoming shout.

"Get your stuff!" Charlie beams shaking his head as he slides to a halt on the kitchen linoleum. "You're not going to believe this," Charlie speaks a mile-a-minute in his excitement. "We got him! Well, we don't got 'im, got 'im yet. I just know where he is." Charlie is almost giddy. He paces as he tries to explain, "He's in Veblen! Skip's Uncle Titus called a few days ago about a squatter in an abandoned, boarded-up house in the Veblen community housing project." Charlie pauses his pacing a moment, frowns as he inspects Agent Brown, but then resumes his pacing again. "I just blew it off." Charlie waves his hand as if shooing a bug. "Uncle Titus is kinda...unique. Quirky." Charlie laughs loudly. "He always wants to talk to me. He's very concerned with nepotism regarding Skip and all. Anyhoo, lo and behold, I finally called him back just now over lunch, and he said he saw a guy push a motorcycle into the boarded-up house. Couple different times. It's him! It's got to be Elliot!"

Austin calmly sips his coffee. He eyes Charlie a moment. Charlie stops pacing, "Are you ok...you know."

Austin holds out his hand. "Steady as a rock. Cold turkey the last two and a half days."

Charlie looks Austin up and down suspiciously before he's satisfied enough to shrug. "Come on. I got a plumber's van as camouflage. Nixon Pluming lets us borrow one of their junkers for covert operations from time to tome." Charlie grins like the Cheshire cat. "We're going to get 'im, Austin." He claps his hands together and rubs them. He beams at the thought.

Chapter 49
Only One

Veblen, South Dakota

Veblen makes up one of the seven political districts on the Sisseton-Wahpeton, a.k.a. Lake Traverse Indian Reservation. The town of Veblen is home to a number of enrolled members, some keep residence in a Housing and Urban Development (HUD) funded public housing project. Located on the southwest corner in the town of Veblen, the tribal housing project is comprised of two square blocks of houses, about two dozen all told. The well-kempt neighborhood has, one and only one, blighted property. A partially burned out, boarded-up house sits kitty-corner from Titus Korman's home in the Veblen community.

Not one to keep quiet, Titus called the BIA Police immediately upon seeing a stranger enter the boarded-up building. A week later, the police are on the scene, albeit, summoning the authorities required multiple calls, including Titus reluctantly calling his nephew. Nonetheless, Charlie and Austin are in Titus' driveway. The Nixon Plumbing van is an ideal vehicle for an undercover operation. Nixon Plumbing is a contracted local firm that routinely makes calls on the tribal housing projects. It would not draw a second glance from neighbors or anyone else for that matter.

Dismounting from the work van, Charlie and Austin walk up the driveway to the front door, passing the rotting, rusted car body in the front yard.

"Love the landscaping," Austin comments with a side glance to the old Dodge.

"Easy," Charlie warns. "We're guests here."

Easing to the front door, the two men clad in work coveralls and toting toolboxes, take in their surroundings. Charlie knocks on the door.

"Did you notice the boarded-up house as we drove by?" Charlie questions.

"Sure did. We'll have a good view from Titus' back windows."

The front door opens a crack after a series of deadbolts are unlocked. Titus peers around the door and recognizes Charlie. He closes the door and a final chain is unhooked. "Come in, come in," he orders, swinging the door wide open.

Titus Korman is eighty years old. He is stooped, thin, and sports a white shock of hair akin to that of a mad scientist. Today's attire is a baggy, long-sleeved western shirt, blue jeans, and suspenders to keep the trousers from slipping and falling to the floor. "Charlie LeBeau," Titus calls out loudly after he closes the door. "How are you?"

He extends his hand and Charlie grabs it, pulling the old man in for a hug. "I'm great, thanks to you." Charlie releases the senior citizen from his grasp and sweeps his hand in the direction of Austin. "This is FBI Special Agent Austin Brown."

Austin steps forward and shakes the man's hand. "Pleased to meet you, sir." Austin bows cordially.

"What, no hug?" Titus questions, punctuating the comment with a raspy laugh.

Austin shoots a glance at Charlie, who seems taken aback by the joke, but finally chortles. "Regular, Shecky Green here, Charlie," Austin drawls.

"I'm sorry for the hug, Titus," Charlie is beaming. "You've located a very bad man. We've been looking all over for him."

"Really?" Titus cocks his head.

"You remember the Deer Slayer?" Charlie frowns. "It was back a couple years ago. He killed a couple kids, kidnapped another from Milbank. But that kid got away."

Titus' eyes narrow, a difficult task with his wrinkled skin. "I remember. He skinned those kids."

Charlie nods confirmation. "He's back." Charlie points. "In that house right over there...at least that's what all signs point to."

Titus moves to the back patio sliding door. He parts the mostly closed blind. "Hmmph," he grunts.

"This is perfect," Austin pipes up. We have surveillance from right here. We don't even need the van."

"Is he still in the house?" Charlie questions. "Uncle Titus, do you know if he's still in the house?"

"As far as I know. That motorcycle makes a helluva racket. You'll hear him if goes."

The conversation is interrupted by a cat tearing from one end of the house to the other. "Jesus Christ!" Austin cries out as he jumps back from the commotion. "What was that?" he exclaims, looking back and forth from Charlie to Titus.

Titus laughs, slapping his knee. "That's just old Chompers. He doesn't like a lot of ruckus, or any visitors for that matter."

Austin's cheeks puff out as he blows a sigh of relief. "I was almost ready to reach for my gun." Austin winks at the old man and he begins to peel off his coveralls revealing his black S.W.A.T. uniform. Charlie follows suit, revealing his camo, duck hunting clothing. Austin makes a face of disapproval at Charlie. "Different sort of huntin' tonight. Looks like I have the right camouflage this time. This will be better'n shootin' all those ducks."

Austin winks again at Charlie, while he retrieves a sawed-off shotgun with a pistol grip. "Hey, turns out I do have a shotgun." Austin feeds shells into the magazine and works the pump action. "Not really a duck huntin' gun though."

Charlie grunts disapproval at Austin's comedic stylings, "Now who's the comedian?"

Titus grabs Charlie's sleeve. "You been shootin' some ducks?"

Austin fields the question. "Pshhh, you should have seen the mess of ducks me and his nephew had to clean." He holds up his hand thigh high. "I'm not kidding, ducks this deep."

Titus turns back to Charlie. "Think you could spare one for an old man? I love roast duck."

Charlie claps a hand on Titus's back. "After we get this guy, you'll have as many ducks as you want. I promise."

Austin works through his gear, checking a headlamp's battery, clicking through all its settings. The backup headlamp is tested. The toolbox of gear makes Austin look like a kid in a candy story. He's calm and relaxed, preparing for tonight's action. "Charlie." He barely looks up as he thumbs rounds off his spare clip for his .45 caliber pistol. "Why don't you get some sleep? I'll keep an eye out. We're looking at a 2:00 am op right? He won't know what hit 'im."

Charlie turns his attention from Titus. "2:00 am? Sounds fine. We getting reinforcements or what?"

"I'm not callin' in backup. We're going to keep this operation small. Less chance tipping Elliot off and less chance of collateral damage."

Austin points the now-empty clip in his hand toward Titus. He begins to load rounds into the clip deliberately. "We got Titus if we need backup."

He looks up wryly at Charlie and chuckles. He's in a good mood. This is his wheelhouse. Planning and executing an attack. Just what the doctor ordered.

"If you think that's best." Charlie grimaces. "I gotta let Skip know what's going on. He can at least muster some folks to be on call if necessary."

Austin points a finger at Charlie, "That reminds me. Tell him to get ready to alert the media. As soon as we capture this guy, we're going full media blitz, tooting our horns. I mean, you are. I'm still technically suspended."

Charlie nods, turning his attention back to Titus, "Ok, Titus, you can go about your business...just don't go outside." Charlie laughs apologetically.

"No plans to." Titus shrugs. "Jeopardy, Wheel of Fortune, the News, and supper. Hey, you guys want anything to eat?"

Austin is all over the food question. "We got you covered, Titus. We got some sub sandwiches from Teal's. Help yourself." He extracts a plastic grocery bag and tosses it on the table.

"How about coffee?" Titus offers.

"Sure," Austin quickly accepts the proposal as he continues to inventory his gear. He flips across his bundle of plastic, zip-tie wrist restraints, pausing for a moment as he ticks through them, counting five in his bag. "You know what? I'm going to put the coveralls back on and go outside. We should make it look like plumbers are working here. Leave some lights on. I'll go out with the water shut-off tool and pretend to turn the water off."

"I like that idea." Charlie extracts his phone and turns to their host. "Titus, you got a guestroom I can crash in?"

Titus points toward the room in which Chompers disappeared. The cat is peeking from under the bed. Charlie gives a wave. "Thanks." He scrolls through his phone. "I gotta give your nephew a call and tell him what's going on."

In the guest bedroom, Charlie lies down and presses the send button on his phone. His body sinks into the star quilt on the bed. It is comfortable, relaxing. The phone rings, trying to connect on Skip's end, and Charlie waits. He looks around the room at the neat, modestly decorated room. One black and white 8 x 10 photo, with tasteful matting and frame, hangs on the wall. It is a portrait of Chief Standing Buffalo.

Charlie studies the reproduction of the professional photo taken probably in the 1860's. Titus is the unofficial historian of the tribe, and his honoring Standing Buffalo deviates from what might be considered the obvious choice, the most famous chief of his people, Chief Red Iron.

Skip finally answers his phone just before it transfers to voicemail. Charlie speaks with a smile plastered on his face. His voice exudes his mood, "You're never gonna believe this, Skip." Charlie listens. "Nope, we're up in Veblen at your Uncle Titus'. Your uncle was calling about a squatter in town. Across from him in the housing project. You remember, I think it was the Duncan house, it partially burned and is sitting here, boarded-up?" Charlie listens on the phone, "Yeah. Well, our squatter is none other than Elliot. Titus saw him wheel the motorcycle inside."

Charlie pulls the phone from his ear. The shout of "No way!" on the other end of the line makes Charlie flinch and he listens to his captain.

"No, no. Just me and Agent Brown. I don't want an army of law enforcement compromising our element of surprise. We're going to take him at 2:00 am. He'll be asleep. We're camped out here at Titus'. I brought our undercover Nixon Plumbing van, so we're good." Charlie listens some more. "Yeah, yeah. I'll give you a call to send the cavalry after we got 'im cuffed. Get your phone number for the press ready. I'm sure WDAY and KELO would love to send cameras. Maybe CNN."

There's a nervous, false bravado in Charlie's tone as laughs at Skip's response. "Hey, I almost forgot to ask. Do you know if there was a reward for the Deer Slayer? There's got to be, right?" Charlie listens. "Yeah, I'll ask Austin. Maybe your uncle is in line for some money." Charlie laughs. "Thanks, Skip. Standby for an early morning wake up call. I'll see you later."

Chapter 50
1:48 a.m.

Charlie emerges from the guest bedroom with a yawn and a stretch. He moves into the dark kitchen where Agent Austin Brown peers through the mostly-closed blind of the patio door. "Did you get some rest?"

Charlie yawns and stretches again. "Fresh as a spring rain."

"He's in there." Austin dips his head toward the house across the street. "I could see a sliver a light coming through a gap in the boards over that window. It just went out. Let's give him another hour."

Charlie and Austin both look to the green LED clock on the kitchen stove. It shows 12:14 am. "You think an hour will be enough for him to fall into deep sleep?" Charlie questions.

"Hour, hour and a half. He'll be asleep. He's dying. I'm predicting it won't be much of a fight, but I'm ready if he wants to brawl. It's been a long time comin'." Austin's brow furrows in the dim light from a lamp located at the far side of the living room. He glances at Charlie. "You ok?"

"I have to admit I'm a little nervous," Charlie states matter-of-factly.

"Good," Austin replies. "If you weren't a little scared, you wouldn't be a normal human being. We got this."

"Think we should have moved the van?" Charlie queries.

"Nah. Darkness has us covered." Austin stares out the window toward the suspect's house.

The men are in near darkness, trying to avoid any attention or suspicion of lights on in the house at this late hour. "Titus asleep?" Charlie questions.

Austin's head nods in affirmation. "Titus hung tough until ten o'clock. He was giving me a history lesson on the tribe. Very interesting. He watched the news and went to bed. He's an interesting man."

"Why don't you relax a bit? I'll keep watch," Charlie offers.

"Sounds good. I'm gonna strap my gear on, then you can get ready, and I'll watch again."

"You want to close your eyes and just get a quick nap?"

Austin waves away the question. "Psssh. I'm too pumped. I'm ready to end this." Austin stands and offers his lookout chair to Charlie.

"You and me both, brother." Charlie maneuvers into the chair and looks out the window into the darkness. He continues speaking without looking away from the window. "Skip's on notice. As soon as we got Elliot secure, and I let him know, he's calling your office and the South Dakota Department of Criminal Investigation. Finally, he'll contact the TV stations."

Austin chuckles as he prepares himself. He smears black makeup on his cheeks. "You want to be on TV, Charlie?"

"I was hoping to get Veronica back on. She loved that stuff when CNN needed some reporting on the priest. Remember that?"

"How could I forget?" Austin finishes darkening his face and nudges Charlie with the face paint. "Get yourself some."

Charlie opens the makeup container and dabs on the dull covering grease, wiping the excess on the back of his hands.

*   *   *

Time passes and the men ready themselves, strapping gear to their bodies. The clock on the kitchen stove changes to 1:48. "You got everything you need?" Austin questions, pulling on his black leather gloves.

"Yup."

Austin sticks out his hand. "Good luck to us."

Charlie grasps the hand in the dim light. "Definitely. Good luck to us."

Chapter 51
Take Down

Less than a block from Uncle Titus' house sits the target. Charlie and Austin move deliberately through the harsh shadows. The streetlight at the end of the block illuminates a small corner of the community, but it is a token security symbol. A dog barks in the distance and the men freeze. Silence settles and the men move to the deeper shadows of the partially-enclosed attached carport of the burned out house. "This side door is where Titus said he saw him move the motorcycle inside," Charlie whispers.

Austin pushes on the plywood covering the door opening. It is loose. "Any chance he's got some sort of booby trap or alarm?" Austin whispers.

Charlie's head shakes slowly, only a silhouette to Austin in the shadows. "Not likely. Who does he think might be onto him? Nobody."

Austin holds a finger to his lips and points at the board covering the door opening. He motions Charlie to move back. He grabs the chunk of plywood and it slips away from its nails without a sound. Austin silently eases the board to the ground. Behind the plywood is a door with a window. Austin flips down his night vision goggles and switches them on. He peers through the door's window. He turns back to Charlie and whispers, "He's got some cans set up as a makeshift alarm. Get your goggles on and we'll go in."

The door has no knob or hardware and Austin puts only the slightest pressure on the door and it moves. The motion causes a low squeak, barely audible to the men even at their close distance. Austin freezes. "Oil," Austin barely breathes the word.

Charlie digs a tiny vial from his chest pocket. He uncaps the tiny eye dropper-like bottle containing mineral oil and directs a squeeze of oil onto each hinge through the tiny gap of the open door, just enough to access the hinges. Austin counts off thirty seconds to himself and then presses on the door. There is no creak from hinges and the men squeeze inside, guns drawn. Night vision goggles reveal a formation of aluminum cans, a makeshift warning device that might detect a clumsy trespasser. The intruders navigate past the cans on the floor.

The men move stealthily through the living room and down the hall, weapons at the ready. The location of their prey is given away by deep breaths of a man asleep. The hunters move through the open door of the back bedroom where Austin had earlier noted the light through a boarded-up window. It is an anticlimactic scene. "Do not move!" Austin shouts the words as he flips up his night vision goggles and clicks on the powerful mini Maglite attached to his .45 caliber pistol.

The groggy captive is blinded by the light and shields his eyes with his hand a moment, stunned by the invaders. Charlie flips up his goggles and slings his pistol-grip shotgun over his shoulder as he leaps on top of Elliot wrapped in his sleeping bag on the floor.

Charlie can feel that there is nothing left of this man as he falls on top of him and leans on him with all his weight. Elliot is completely submissive and Charlie flips him on his stomach with a grunt and a low groan from the prisoner.

"You are under arrest." Austin growls the words.

Charlie looks back to Austin, "You got the restraints?"

Austin touches his chest with his free hand, holding the gun with its light trained on Charlie and the Deer Slayer. "I'm sorry, Charlie. I don't got 'em. They're back at the house in my gear. In the toolbox."

Charlie feels the pocket in his vest where his handcuffs should be. They are not there. Removed by Austin while Charlie slept, this was part of Austin's plan. Charlie digs his knee into Elliot's back, angry at this situation. "You don't have anything? Not even a zip-tie?"

"No. You're going to have to go get 'em. I got him covered. Go!"

Charlie hesitates. This is the scenario that nagged at him. It had been in the back of his mind for weeks…Agent Brown alone with Elliot.

"Give me the gun. I'll hold him. You go."

Austin snorts a laugh. "That's not the way this works, Charlie."

"I don't think…"

"Just go!" An agitated Agent Brown shouts, causing both Elliot and Charlie to flinch.

Charlie manhandles Elliot out of the sleeping bag and pushes him to his knees, "Put your hands up," he orders.

Charlie digs a mini Maglite from his pocket as he gets to his feet and backs out of the room. He clicks the light on and shines it on Elliot. He is on his knees, hands in the air dressed only in his boxers. He is emaciated and the intense light seems to accentuate the scars on his torso. Elliot has seemed to regain his senses and he smirks at the source of the light. "I won't resist." The words from the man cause both Charlie and Austin to stiffen.

"Austin…don't do it." Charlie's words are flat.

"Nothing's goin to happen. Just get the cuffs!" Austin shouts the order, his body rocks, feeding off the adrenaline. "Go!"

Charlie pauses only a moment before breaking into a trot down the hallway, crashing through the aluminum cans and out of the house. He sprints across the street, his flashlight leading the way. He digs for his phone as he runs, hobbling a bit, trying to extract the phone. Finally freeing the phone, he powers it on as he enters Titus' house as quietly as possible.

He is in and out of the house, grabbing a pair of handcuffs from Austin's toolbox. He checks the phone as he leaves the house. He has service and he presses the button to call Skip. The phone goes to voicemail after a series of rings. Charlie ends the call and dials again as he jogs back across the street. Skip picks up. "Skip. Send the cavalry! We got 'im!"

* * *

In the back bedroom of the house, Austin holds the pistol on Elliot. The pathetic looking man with bald head and beard reminds Austin of the Unabomber, Ted Kaczynski, sans the hair. He looks crazy, smiling back

into the blazing beam of light. Elliot moves from his knees to a cross-legged position. "Did I say you could move?"
Austin shouts the words. "Lace your fingers behind your head."

Elliot does as ordered. "I'm a dead man. You'd be doing me a favor if you shot me right now."

"Just give me a second. You'll have your wish." Austin eases a step closer, just out of reach of his prisoner. He feels his pocket with his free hand, checking for his keys. "Lower your hands."

A puzzled Elliot drops his hands from behind his head, but still holds them at shoulder height. "Austin smiles down at him, "I can't shoot you in the head and blow one of your fingers off without suspicions. Just in case you're wondering." Elliot cocks his head, not understanding at first, but then he smiles. "Just one question," Austin asks softly. "Why my wife?"

Elliot grimaces at the question, opening and closing his mouth. "She was an easy target. You thought you and your family were safely tucked away." Elliot shrugs, "Before you shoot me, can you do something for me?" Austin shakes his head in refusal. "Well, I'm going to just tell you a couple things anyway. You don't have to listen." Elliot's voice is a whisper as realizes his time is limited. "There's more of my work to be uncovered." Elliot sighs, "Tell Charlie there's something coming to him after I'm dead." He shakes his head, coming back to his reality, "I didn't answer the question about your wife. I'm sorry." Elliot grins maniacally, finally answering the question with his own question, "Why not?"

Elliot's last words are eclipsed by the roaring report of the pistol. The bullet between his eyes rips the back of Elliot's head apart. He slowly tips over, eyes unclosed, listing to the left before sprawling face down on the floor.

Austin works quickly to remove his keys from his pocket. He fumbles to detach the mini-Stanley utility knife from the key ring his trembling hands finally cooperate enough to accomplish the task. He exposes the blade of the knife sliding the locking tab forward as he kneels next to Elliot's body. He presses the knife into Elliot's hand, and he curls the dead hand's fingers around the utility knife. He raises the hand and drops it. It falls with a thud, the knife bouncing from the hand into a pool of gathering blood. Austin steps back from the body, staring down, cocking his head to view the scene, admiring his work, self satisfied. He whispers, "It is finished, Jeannie."

*   *   *

Outside the house, Charlie bounces across the street, happy. Relieved. Trotting on cloud nine. The gunshot stops him in his tracks. He whispers into the phone, "Gotta go." He ends the call, cutting off Skip as he shouts repeatedly, "What was that?"

Charlie cautiously enters the house, easing carefully through the cans scattered on the floor. He unslings the shotgun from his shoulder, every sense on edge. In the back bedroom, Charlie can see a light moving. He clicks off his flashlight and he continues to sneak forward. He reaches the doorway and lowers his weapon with one hand, the other hand raises his mini-Maglite and he clicks it on. He aims the beam on the body, blood still oozing from the gaping wound and exposed brains of Elliot. His flashlight's beam is scattered, reflecting eerily off the pool of blood expanding before his eyes. Charlie's head shakes as he locks eyes with Austin. "He had a knife," Austin grunts the words without conviction.

Charlie's shoulders slump.

Chapter 52
Statement

For Charlie, it's an interminable wait for the rest of his fellow law enforcement comrades to arrive. It is a long, quiet interlude. The silence under the streetlight is periodically interrupted by the slight rustle of leaves drifting across the street in the breeze. Multiple times Austin begins to recount what happened, but Charlie halts him. "Just wait. I can't take your statement. You're going to have to explain it to Skip, or someone else. I didn't actually witness the shooting."

Austin is hurt by what he deems a lack of support from Charlie, but not hurt enough to stop smiling. He beams. His nemesis is dead. He has fulfilled his promise to kill that man. His mix of emotions over the death of a fellow human being is offset by his satiated revenge. Right or wrong on the shooting, he will have to live with it. He knows there is zero chance anyone will say anything negative about the outcome of the operation, even if they have suspicions. Austin begins his story again, to

Charlie's objection. This time he doesn't stop. Austin recalls the shooting aloud, whether Charlie wants to hear it or not.

It's about an hour later when the first sirens and lights appear in the distance. Charlie puts his arm around Austin's shoulder. "I'm glad it's over. I got your back. Just tell them what happened and I'll tell them what happened. It's going to be as simple as that."

The men stand under the streetlight like actors on the stage, illuminated by a spotlight. Austin smiles. "I know you do, buddy. No worries." He shrugs, "Feel kinda weird. Closure." He shakes his head with a somewhat bewildered expression. "Now what?" He laughs uncomfortably.

"Here they come." Charlie gives a nod to the east as the sirens are silenced, but the strobing, flashing, red and blue lights pulse in the darkness. The first wave of law enforcement is the Roberts County Sheriff's Office. Two deputies, each in separate patrol cars, pull up next to the boarded-up house. Charlie waves his arms as the men scramble from their cars, weapons drawn. The men catch the signal and relax.

Skip is just a minute behind the deputies and he spots Charlie and Austin under the streetlight. He pulls up next to Charlie and Austin on the corner and rolls down his window. "Since I see you standing here with no prisoner, I'm going to assume we have a body." Charlie nods. "I have first responders coming. I heard the shot over the phone and when you said, 'gotta go' I figured something went bad." Skip continues. "The question I have is, how bad?"

Charlie responds, his tone is muted, "Dead."

"Who's the shooter?" Skip looks to Charlie.

Charlie jerks his head toward Austin.

Skip nods. "Austin, why don't you step into my mobile command unit." Skip finally has a hint of emotion in his voice. "I guess I'm the on-scene commander. I'll get your statement. You're next Charlie."

Charlie forces a grin. "You know what? Let me go tell Titus what's going on. We've just been waiting outside. I'll let him know before this place is a total zoo."

Skip nods and Charlie trudges back to Uncle Titus' house.

In an hour the streets of Veblen are flooded by twenty-five-plus emergency vehicles. A few neighbors peek out their windows, a couple come outside to catch a glimpse of the activities, but most ignore the situation.

Forty-five minutes later Austin exchanges places with Charlie. He heads to Titus' house to gather his gear, while Charlie sits next to Skip in his BIA Police Tahoe providing his account of the operation. It's a fairly short conversation, filling a page in Skip's notebook, compared to four pages of notes from Austin.

After their separate statements, Charlie and Austin are together with Skip. "Do you need my weapon?" Austin asks.

"Yeah," Skip replies. "Protocol." He pulls a plastic bag from his console and opens it. "Drop it in."

Austin pulls his pistol from its holster, drops the clip, and ejects a cartridge from the chamber. "The empty is still in the house." He drops the clip, the cartridge, and the pistol into the bag.

"We'll find it," Skip assures. Skip pulls a Sharpie from his pocket and annotates the evidence bag.

"Just think," Austin announces. "How much money I saved the government."

Austin grins, but Charlie has a frown to match. "Yeah," Charlie replies unconvincingly.

"There's O'Malley from DCI." Skip points toward the carport. "I'm going to go check in with him. Then I'll see about looking at the scene. Good job, men. It's good to get a killer off the streets." Skip extends his hand to Charlie, who shakes it. He extends his hand to Agent Brown. "Sorry it had to end this way." Skip grimaces as Austin grasps his hand. "Why don't you guys head out. You've had a long night. I'll handle everything until tomorrow."

"Thanks, Skip," Austin's voice is husky. His energy has faded with the adrenaline. "I'm just glad it's over."

Chapter 53
Aftermath

Veronica's Old House

It's evening; Austin sits at the kitchen table drinking coffee. Next to him is Dominique, his algebra homework spread out on the table. He pushes his paper toward Austin. "Is that right?"

Austin glances over his cup as he sips coffee. "Ok. Everything is procedurally correct, but what did you forget?"

Dom's eyes narrow as he stares at the paper and shrugs. Austin taps his finger on the worksheet. "Negative sign!" Dom slaps a hand to his forehead. "Dang it!"

"Details. Details," Austin chides.

A knock on the front door interrupts. "Come in!" Austin shouts from the table.

Charlie enters carrying a plastic grocery bag. "I brought some leftovers." Charlie notices Dom sitting with Austin at the table. "Oh. Hey, you got company. Sorry to disturb."

Austin waves away the apology. "Whatever. Charlie, do you know Dominique Thompson?"

"Sure. Hey, Dom."

"Hi, Sergeant LeBeau," Dom pipes up.

"What are you working on?" Charlie questions as he sets the bag on the counter.

"Algebra."

Austin points to Dom. "The kid here is doing some work for me. Got the leaves all raked up. Now I'm trying to help him with some math."

"Good, good," Charlie notes. "I saw the yard. Nice work. It's no joke raking all those leaves." Charlie looks in the bag to remind him of what they had for supper. "I brought some food, well, Veronica sent it. Some pork chops. Rice. Biscuits."

Austin smiles guiltily. "We had A&W earlier." He glances to Dom and back to Charlie. "But, I could probably eat again." He winks at Dom.

"Sounds good to me," Dom concurs pushing his homework aside.

"Finish your math...then we eat." Austin taps the table with his finger.

Dom begrudgingly pulls the papers back in front of him.

"I gotta go." Charlie waves. "Veronica wants to watch a movie." Charlie turns toward the front door, but stops. "One other thing." Charlie faces Austin. "You mind coming by the office tomorrow? Get your weapon and talk?"

"No problem. Morning? Afternoon? What works for you?"

Charlie purses his lips. "Morning. I'll see you then. Good night. See you, Dom."

"See you tomorrow," Austin calls out as Charlie exits, pulling the front door closed behind him.

"Man that food smells good." Austin stands. "C'mon, man. Hurry up and finish that homework."

Chapter 54
Insurance

BIA Police Headquarters – Sisseton, South Dakota

The debriefing is over. Charlie and Austin sit across from Skip at his desk. The door is closed and Skip leans back in his chair, clasping his hands behind his head. "What are you going to do now?" Skip leans forward. "Oh, by the way." He bends down and opens a drawer.

Austin watches the captain as he responds. "Believe me, I've been giving it a lot of thought. I've decided I'll resign from the FBI and head back east...once everything is all clear."

"Well, here you go." Skip hands back the bag containing Austin's pistol, ammo, and clip. "All clear as far as we're concerned. Legitimate shoot. Just heard back from the Assistant U.S. Attorney."

"Wow. Less than a week." Austin chuckles. "They're dropping this case like a hot potato. Close that file and get it off my desk! I can just hear their battle cry." Austin puts a hand to his ear, pantomiming. "Guess I'll turn in my papers then." He smiles and Charlie and Skip notice.

"Look at this guy," Skip directs his comment to Charlie. "Like the weight of the world is off his shoulders. You gonna retire?"

Austin shakes his head. "Too young."

"Just quittin'?" Skip asks with concern.

"I'm about eight years from a pension." Austin frowns. "I'm not gonna make it. Besides, my wife left me and the kids set up with her life insurance. I don't need the money."

"Really?" Charlie questions, taken aback by the statement.

"Get a load of this guy." Austin gives Skip a look, "Somebody's not up to speed with his life insurance." Skip chuckles. Austin puts a hand on Charlie's shoulder. "You're a married man now, Charlie. You got Nat and Claude. What if something happens to you, God forbid? Tell 'im, Skip."

Skip reluctantly nods in agreement. "Jeannie had two million dollars tied up in a couple policies for herself. We had it figured that if something did happen to her…" Austin's voice loses steam and trails off. Charlie returns the favor, placing a comforting hand on Austin's shoulder, "Anyway, the kids have trust funds now."

"You said you're goin' back East then?" Skip inquires.

"Yup. Back to Indianapolis to be near Jeannie's folks. They're going to help with the girls. Actually, I'll be assisting them. We're going to share custody."

"That's nice," Skip comments softly. "It's good to have help. Family. They'll be alright."

Austin stands with a groan and a sigh. "I'm going to take off."

Charlie stands. "I'll walk you out."

The men exit the building, each lost in his own thoughts. They stroll to Austin's car in uncomfortable silence. Standing a moment beside his car Austin mumbles. "This is it then."

"You headin' back to Pierre?" Charlie kicks at the pavement.

"Yeah, in a few days. I'll get Veronica's house straightened out. Then get the house in Pierre prepped and put on the market."

"What about Dom?"

"Oh, yeah," Austin's tone is earnest. "We're going to stay in touch. I met with his foster parents. We worked out a deal. If they want he can come visit in the summers and if he buckles down, stays in school, and out of trouble, I'll help him out. Keeps his grades up, I told him I'd provide some spending money. If he graduates, I'll put him through college. Master's too, if he so desires. I really think he can do it."

"Wow." Charlie's eyes widen and he flinches back. "That's very generous."

"He's a good kid, just troubled family. No family. Reminds me of someone." Austin forces a half-hearted smile.

"Yeah." Charlie clucks his tongue. "Too many like him on the reservation. I'm gonna see if Nat can catch up with him and talk about playing some ball, and some sort of sports. It's a good activity and provides a distraction and some discipline."

"That's a great idea." Austin nods along with Charlie. "I might mention it to Dom."

"Before I forget." Charlie holds up his finger as he remembers his reason for walking Austin to his car. "What are you doing for supper tomorrow night?"

Austin frowns deeply. "No plans. Why, you buying?"

"As a matter of fact, yes. At the casino. I'd like you to be there. It's sorta a celebration." Charlie smiles weakly. "You know, after all this." Charlie throws his hands up. "We gotta blow off some steam."

"No doubt." Austin opens his car door. "I'll be there." He climbs in his car and repeats himself, "I'll be there. What time?"

"Seven. We got a room in the back reserved."

Austin nods, slams the door, and starts the engine. Charlie recognizes the muffled song emanating from the car. It's "The Reason" by Hoobastank. Austin gives a thumbs up to a waving Charlie as he pulls out of the lot.

Chapter 55
Announcements

Charlie's House

Nat stands in the doorway of his room. He stares at the bed, but his mind is far away, drifting back in time to a couple years ago. He remembers staring at his empty bedroom after cleaning out his old house after his mom died. He remembers the surreal feeling of trying to pick up his life and relocate it to here, here with his Uncle Charlie and Grandpa. He had survived those darkest days. The day of the funeral, the day after that, then the next day. The days came and went and things got better. He had recovered after the loss of his mother. This decision is nothing compared to that.

Charlie's voice calls from the living room, "Come on, everyone. We have a reservation!"

Nat snaps out of his trance-like memories. A twisted, satisfied smile crosses his face as he moves into the living room, and Charlie notices. "What's up with you?"

"Nothing," Nat counters defensively.

"Well, you're all grinning like the proverbial cat that swallowed the canary."

"I am? Sorry." Nat shrugs an apology.

"C'mon!" Charlie calls out again.

Claude appears from the bathroom. "Keep your pants on."

Veronica scurries from the master bedroom. "Sorry, sorry, sorry," she repeats on every bouncing, trotting step. "We taking my car?"

"Yeah," Charlie sighs a grumbling sigh. "It's the only one that fits us all."

"When you getting one of those fancy double-cab trucks? It'd be awesome for huntin.'" Nat questions as they all exit the house and trudge down the patio steps.

"Hmmm," Charlie contemplates, tapping a finger on his chin dramatically, "I guess when I win the lottery. We got your college to pay for."

"I'm on scholarship," Nat counters. "Plus, my mom left me some money."

"That's right." Charlie's voice goes higher. "You want to give me that money? I'll buy a new truck, you can have my old one."

"I'm not going to dignify that question with an answer," Nat replies, emphasizing his words like a seasoned politician.

They all load up in Veronica's Ford Explorer with Veronica behind the wheel. "Look." Nat leans forward from his position in the backseat. "Even Veronica has a nice, modern vehicle. Four-wheel drive. It's awesome."

"Put your seatbelt on," Charlie orders. "I don't need a new hunting vehicle; I got this one as a backup if needed."

"Like heck you do," Veronica joins the conversation.

"Just checking to see if you're listening." Charlie pats his wife's knee as she drives.

It's a short drive to Sisseton and over to the Dakota Connection along Interstate 29. The overhead lights of the parking lot and the casino sign illuminate the night as the group enters the casino to find Kelli waiting for them at the hostess' stand. She provides a welcoming hug to Veronica. "Hello, everyone," she calls out with a wave.

Lacey Michaels, the hostess, greets everyone, "It'll be just a couple minutes. Hi, Charlie. I think Courtney wants to talk to you."

"Sure, Lacey. Can you tell her we're here?"

Austin arrives and joins the group. "There he is. My hero." Veronica hugs Austin.

"How are you?" Austin questions.

"I'm fine. I don't think you've met my co-editor, this is Kelli Burnbaugh."

Kelli steps forward and extends her hand. "Oooh, this is good news, sounds like I just got promoted. Co-editor! Hi, how are you?" She shakes Austin's hand.

"Hi, I'm Austin Brown."

"He's an FBI agent," Veronica adds.

"Not for much longer," Austin chuckles.

"Oh?" Veronica questions.

"Yeah, I'm hanging it up. I've had enough." Austin shakes hands with Claude and Nat. "You gotta know when to say when."

"Ok, let's go. I'm ready to eat," Claude urges.

"Not yet, Dad. Wait until the hostess is ready for us."

Courtney appears. "Party of six for LeBeau?" She flashes a welcoming grin. "Please, follow me. We have a special room for your party."

"Party?" Claude echoes the word.

"Dad, she means group," Charlie grumbles.

Just off the main dining area a larger room for about twenty-five people is set up for eight. Courtney leads the way and the group is followed by Lacey, who has picked up two bottles of champagne. Courtney's two kids are already seated at the table. Lacey jams the champagne bottles into the ice coolers on the table. "What's going on?" a confused Claude questions.

"You'll find out." Charlie pats his dad's shoulder. "We're having a bit of a celebration."

"Please, everyone, find your seats," Courtney takes over. "There are name placards at each place setting. Take your seat and Lacey will get your drink orders and bring your salads."

The group sorts out the seating arrangements. Charlie sits, Veronica on one side, Britney on the other. He touches the top of the little girl's head gently with his hand, and Britney smiles. A still puzzled Claude questions again loudly, "What are we doing here?" It dawns on him as he quietly answers his own question and tries to not draw attention. "Oh, yeah." He beams with pride.

Charlie stands and takes a drink of water. "Today we are celebrating. Celebrating lots of stuff. First off, Courtney has officially added a new edition to her family, Haley."

The group around the table applauds. "On top of that, I have some other great personal news to share. A couple of you in this room already know." Charlie gives a wink to his dad. He puts a hand on Britney's shoulder. "During the last couple months I found out that this young lady is my daughter."

Gasps resound from Nat, Austin, and Kelli, while Claude is the lone person awkwardly applauding. Charlie leans down and hugs the little girl. "It's gonna take some getting used to, for both of us, but I am so happy to have Brittney." Charlie looks to Veronica. "Stepdaughter." His eyes shift to Claude. "Granddaughter." And finally his eyes meet Nat's. "And cousin." Charlie shrugs. "I can't wait to get to know Brittney and the rest of her family, and for Brittney to get to know her new family."

Lacey arrives with another waitress bringing in sparkling grape juice and trays of champagne flutes. "Dad, can you open that bottle of champagne? I'll get this one." Corks fly across the room and glasses are filled. Toasts are made and glasses clink. The salads arrive and Veronica stands. "Before we start to eat, there is one other bit of good news we'd like to share." Veronica pulls Charlie to his feet. "We're going to have a baby!"

Everyone gasps audibly, except for Austin, who enjoys being on the inside this time, and his grin proves it. Courtney is on her feet immediately. "This is wonderful!" She steps forward and puts her hand on Veronica's belly for an instant before wrapping her in a big hug.

Kelli is wagging a finger at Veronica from her seat at the table, shaking her head. She can't contain herself, and she stands and joins the hugging procession surrounding Veronica. "I saw you drinking the sparkling grape juice. And you promoted me to co-editor. It didn't even register!" Her arms flail. "You got me. You fooled me, but now you *really* need me!"

"Well, yeah." Veronica holds Kelli's hand. "And, guess what? We might have a house for you." Veronica tips her glass to Austin, who returns the gesture, tipping his glass of sparkling grape juice in her direction.

Nat stands and taps a spoon on his water glass, drawing everyone's attention. He holds up his glass of sparkling grape juice. "A toast to Uncle Charlie and Veronica...Aunt Veronica."

"Hear, hear!" the group responds and raises glasses.

"I also have an announcement, a much, much smaller announcement, but my timing is impeccable. I am going to enroll early at Black Hills State. We've talked it over and I think it's a good deal." Nat holds up his hands in a shrug. "Plus, what perfect timing. Now you'll have a nursery for the baby." A collective chuckle ripples through the group. "Let's eat!" Nat declares, raising his glass again.

The group laughs and applauds as they find their seats. Soon it is forks clanking off plates as they enjoy salads. The merriment is cut short with a buzz of Charlie's phone from his shirt pocket, "Oh, no." He winces at Veronica as he sees the caller ID, and it's Skip. He puts the phone to his ear. "Hello, Skip."

Charlie listens, stands, and moves away from the table. "Oh, no. I'll come in. Don't worry about it. See ya."

Charlie rejoins the table. "Sorry, Honey. I gotta go. Some duck hunters found some bones."

Claude overhears. "Bones? Where?"

"They were trying to jump-shoot some ducks off the old Kirschner gravel pit, and stumbled on some freshly dug up bones this evening." Charlie's shoulder slump. "I'm sorry."

He kisses Veronica on the top of her head and hugs her. "Can I get your keys? I'll have Nat give me a ride home, and he can come back."

Veronica stands and smiles. "Yeah, no problem. We'll box your meal and bring it home for you." She hands over her keys. "Love you." She raises up on her tip-toes kisses Charlie on the lips.

"Police business!" Charlie announces loudly to the room. "I gotta go, but thanks for coming. Enjoy the food! C'mon, Nat. Give me a ride."

Nat is up and following his uncle out the door. With a wave, Charlie disappears. It's another night on the job as a BIA policeman while overhead the casino speakers softly play Dwight Yoakam's cover of Elvis Presley's famous song "Suspicious Minds."

Greg Heitmann has worked for the Federal Government for 20 plus years, which pays the bills while pursuing a career in writing. His life experiences have been an inspiration for much of his writing. Look for something new from Greg soon!